MW00438354

By Tahir Shah

A Son of a Son
The Clockmaker's Box
Beyond the Devil's Teeth
Casablanca Blues
Casablanca Blues: The Screenplay
Eye Spy
Godman
Hannibal Fogg and the Supreme Secret of Man
House of the Tiger King
In Arabian Nights
In Search of King Solomon's Mines
Jinn Hunter: Book One – The Prism
Jinn Hunter: Book Two – The Jinnslayer
Jinn Hunter: Book Three – The Perplexity
Journey Through Namibia
Paris Syndrome
Scorpion Soup
Sorcerer's Apprentice
The Afghan Notebook
The Anthologies
The Caliph's House
The Middle East Bedside Book
The Reason to Write
Three Essays
Timbuctoo
Timbuctoo: The Screenplay
Trail of Feathers
Travels With Myself
Travels With Nasrudin

GODMAN

TAHIR SHAH

GODMAN

TAHIR SHAH

SECRETUM MUNDI PUBLISHING

MMXX

Secretum Mundi Publishing Ltd
Kemp House
City Road
London
EC1V 2NX
United Kingdom

www.secretum-mundi.com
info@secretum-mundi.com

First published by Secretum Mundi Publishing Ltd, 2020
VERSION 10092020

GODMAN

Visit the author's website at: www.tahirshah.com

ISBN 978-1-912383-53-5

For my godmother,
Clare Maxwell-Hudson, with love

PART I

1

THE BLACKPOOL GRAND had hosted the crème de la crème of entertainment in its time, from vaudeville to full musical extravaganzas, and even pantomime.

In the theatre's long history, none had wowed the audience more artfully, or with such finesse, as the maestro of magical delight – The Great Maharaja Malipasse.

The stalls, dress circles, and the boxes full to capacity, the house lights slowly dimmed, and the royal blue curtains eased apart. Amid an electrifying ambience, the celebrated sorcerer stepped from the shadows into a shaft of dazzling stage light.

The Maharaja was cloaked in an emerald-green opera cape, his head crowned in a magnificent turban, adorned with priceless gems.

In absolute silence, and with the audience lost in speechless anticipation, the magician bowed.

Before him, raised to waist height, was a black coffin, its surface festooned with cryptic symbols in silver and gold.

Channelling an ancient sorcery passed down through generations of his ancestral line, the magician thrust both arms up into the air, his face grizzled with rage.

'By the sacred power of the lost tradition!' he boomed. 'And by the diabolic force of ultimate darkness, I command you to reveal yourself!'

As one, the audience gasped.

Snarling, The Great Maharaja Malipasse stepped back, hands clenched into fists.

A full minute of transfixed anticipation passed.

Unable to take it, a woman fainted at the back.

Another cackled in anguish and in joy.

A man at the front jumped up and screamed out.

Again, the revered magician thrust both fists up in the air, commanding the casket to open.

But it did not.

2

HARRY SINGH UNLOADED three crates of equipment from his battered old transit van, ferrying it inside the village hall.

He looked much older than his thirty-three years, his eyes ringed from fatigue, worry, and stress.

Even before he was over the threshold a stout woman with a cigarette hanging from the corner of her mouth accosted him.

'You're late! The nippers'll be here in a minute!'

'Me mate'll park the van and come round to help set up.'

'Well, get bleedin' cracking!'

'Don't worry, we'll set up fast.'

'You better 'ah, or Bruce'll 'ave your guts for garters!'

'How long shall I do?'

'Till they look like they're sick of ya!'

'How old?' Harry asked.

'It's a sixth birthday party – so they'll be sick of you in no time. Bleedin' easy money if you ask me!'

'Who's the birthday kid?'

The woman rummaged a hand down her blouse and pulled out a crumpled scrap of paper.

'*Millicent*. Sounds like a toff.'

'No problem,' Harry replied, pushing through with the first crate, 'I'll make sure to do something a bit special.'

3

AN HOUR LATER a sea of five- and six-year-old girls was squirming on the floor, waiting for the show to begin.

Seated in a prim party dress in hand-sewn ivory lace, was Millicent. Unlike the other kids she wasn't impressed.

'Mummy!' she called out loud. 'It's draughty in here, and I don't want to catch a cold.'

'Hush there my little strawberry,' a stern woman cooed from the sidelines. 'It'll warm up in a mo!'

Swivelling round, she shot a look of poison at the stout woman who'd been standing at the front. She in turn glared at Harry Singh, who was waiting in the wings.

A moment after that, the performance started.

Head to toe in sequins, an opera cape trailing behind him, The Great Maharaja Malipasse stepped onto the stage.

His expression severe, both hands clenched into fists, he snarled down at the sea of squirming little girls, each one a veritable picture of primness.

'I am a mighty sorcerer!' he boomed. 'And I have the power to turn all of you into wart-covered toads!'

On hearing the words, a clutch of girls at the back began weeping.

'We don't want to be toads!' one sobbed.

'We want to be princesses!' whimpered another.

Reaching over to a stand, the magician grabbed a shoebox and emptied it out onto the boards. A moment later, two dozen toads were jumping about, as the little girls screamed hysterically.

Cackling, the great magician danced about, leering and gesticulating like a ghoul from the depths of Hell.

His face contorted into a wicked expression of rage, he hurled a handful of magic powder at the audience…

Powder that erupted into an explosion of flames.

4

BLACKPOOL'S NORTH PIER was all but deserted, with even the faithful avoiding it in the torrential rain.

At the far end, a bundle of silk and sequins huddled sorrowfully under a torn golfing umbrella, a giant emerald-green turban lopsided on his head.

Staggering from the pier's landward end, a polystyrene cup of milky tea in either hand, came Bitu. The one man who'd stuck by The Great Maharaja Malipasse through thick and thin, there was a dilapidated air about him, as though he was worn out like a pair of leather shoes. Of nebulous age, he could have been anything from thirty to sixty. Like his friend, he'd been reduced to little more than a shell by a series of disastrous events.

'Here ya are,' he mumbled on reaching the magician's pitch. 'There's more acid rain in there than tea, but it was a long walk from that machine. Robbed me twice before it spewed this out.'

'Sure you're not pocketing the change, Bitu-bhai?' Harry snarled.

'Don't you dare doubt me or I'll cuff you!'

'Hate this cold.'

'You're immune to it,' Bitu sniffed. 'Like all the Englishers born here.'

'Immune to what?'

'To the cold and the grey, that's what.'

'What tripe are ya talking now, Bitu-bhai? I'm cursed. You know it full well – the Curse of Harry Houdini!'

Huddling under the umbrella, Bitu let out a painful groan, like the death throes of a bull elephant.

'Don't be so melodramatic!'

'It's my ticker. Can feel it getting ready to tick its last tock. I'll expire right here! Then you'll have a mess on ya hands.'

'More of a mess than I already have?'

'Yeah. A royal flush of stinking crap!'

Unfurling his left hand, Harry jerked away the turban.

'This is the end! Not doing another minute of it!'

'A little bit of rain and you're done?'

'It's not the rain! It's not that!'

'Then what is it?'

'The curse. I'm cursed! That's what I am!'

Bitu looked at his friend, their dripping faces inches from one another.

'O Great Maharaja!' he shot back. 'I'm so sorry Your Majesty has the luxury.'

Wiping the inside of the turban over his face, Harry sat up straight.

'I really do have one. Think about it! First the jammed clasp on the damned casket, then the fireball.'

'The lock was one thing, but the fire…' Bitu's face froze as his mind replayed the memory. 'That was not nice.'

'*Not nice*?! It was frigging demonic. It was the curse!'

'You can't throw it in. We built it all from scratch.'

'Fifteen years flushed down the drain!' Harry yelled. 'Two washed-up has-beens fit for nothing!'

Sucking the mucus from his nasal passages into his throat, Bitu forced a smile.

'Sun will follow rain,' he offered optimistically. 'There'll be a rainbow any minute.'

'Ya talking tosh! This rain's never gonna stop! Even when the rest of Blackpool's bathed in blazing sunshine there'll be two clouds left – one pouring down on you, and the other pouring on me!'

'Harry-bhai, listen to what you're saying. What'd you do if you turn your back on this?!'

Harry's face lit up at the question.

'Dunno!' he cried. 'Haven't a clue! I'm sure a door'll open. Or a pair of doors… or even a whole load of 'em! Doors to Rolls-Royces and palaces, doors to frigging office blocks with my name on the front, doors to castles and even private jets!'

Bitu cleared his nasal passages a second time. Aiming, he spat between the boards, and missed.

'Send me a postcard when you get to Niagara Falls,' he chortled.

'I'm not going to Niagara Falls!'

'Then where you going?'

Harry Singh shoved away the turban and the conjuring props.

'I'm going to find my destiny!'

'Where? Manchester?' Bitu cackled, his sinuses clogged again.

'A million miles from Manchester!'

Clambering to his feet, Harry stormed away, back down the pier, the rain even heavier than before.

'Come back! Help pack up!' Bitu called out.

Drenched to the bone, Harry Singh called back:

'Leave it all! It's friggin' crap. It's a cursed incarnation!'

5

THE DISC-BLADE RIPPED through a sheep's carcass like a

hot knife through butter, cleaving it smartly in two with no trouble at all.

Hunched over the machine, the stub of a cigarette screwed into the corner of his mouth, a black turban wound tight over his head, Fred Singh was thinking about the fifty he had each way on Ghost Boy at Wincanton that afternoon.

His white coat drenched in muck and blood, and a week's beard on his cheeks, he grabbed the right side of the carcass and slung it into an oil drum at the far end of the bench.

The Singh Bros' business motto was *Meat of Wonderful Dreams*! but it would have been more accurate as *Meat of Wretched Nightmares*! The cutting room resembled a battlefield. The floor was strewn with lumps of matted hair, guts, gristle, and bones. There was a cockroach problem, although the rats kept their numbers down – as if they preferred live prey to the offcuts of third-rate meat.

Wiping his bloodied hands over the front of his coat, Fred Singh snatched a cigarette from behind his ear, lit it, and breathed out a plume of smoke.

The door opened and his brother strode in, wearing a leather jacket and jeans.

'Hey Harry! Come to do man's work at last?'

'Nah. Looking for Dad. Seen him?'

'Up in the office. He's doing the accounts.'

'Thanks.'

'Gonna beg him for another loan… for your Great Maharaja Maliponce?'

'*Malipasse*… The Great Maharaja Malipasse! And the answer's NO! I've chucked it all in.'

'What?'

'Yeah. I'm moving on.'

'About time. Well welcome back to the planet Earth!'

'*Pah!*'

'So ya going to join us? Could do with a young man with a degree like yourself.'

His face screwed up in an involuntary spasm, Harry cast an eye over the room.

'What bloody use would a chemistry degree do me in a place like this?! You must be out of your mind. This is the last place on earth I'd come and work!'

'So what's it gonna be?'

'Dunno. Just not magic tricks or rotting meat. That's all I know!'

6

THE OFFICE AT Singh Bros was no more than a mezzanine, a squat cupboard-like space at one end of the meat-cutting room.

Mr Singh Sr liked to be close to where the action was, so he could be certain his four sons were working. Whenever the disc-saw ceased for more than a minute, he'd peer down from the window, scan the battlefield of entrails and gore, and yell X-rated insults at his offspring.

He was doing just that when Harry pushed open the door.

'Hey Papa!'

Ranjit Singh jerked round. A tight black turban above and a long grey beard below, his eyes were small and mistrustful.

'What you here for you good for nothing... you Maharaja Malipam! Made me the laughing stock of Blackpool you did!'

'*Malipasse*, Maharaja Malipasse, and anyway it's gone. Buried and lost.'

'What you talking?'

'The Great Maharaja Malipasse has gone into magical retirement.'

Mr Singh senior's small beady eyes shone like cut diamonds.

'Gone?!'

'Yes.'

'Buried and lost?!'

'Yes, Papa. Buried and lost.'

Palpitating, the elderly butcher held out his arms.

'Oh my boy, my dear beloved black sheep son. Come to me!'

Harry didn't move. His expression hardened.

'I'm not coming into the family business, Pa. I'm not cut out to be cutting chunks of putrid meat.'

'Not putrid! None of it putrid! Is good meat. Best quality! I know your plan, boy! You coming here tricking me, asking for money so you can put the joke green turban back on your stupid head! Why you not wear a fine turban... the turban of our warrior caste?!'

'I was proud to wear the green turban, Pa. It was part of my act. Part of the magic. But, as I've told you, it's all over. And *no* I haven't come for money. I've come for something far more special.'

Ranjit Singh's eyes drilled into those of his youngest son.

'Nothing more special than money!' he roared.

'Yes there is, Pa.'

'What? What you asking for?'

'I'm asking for your blessing.'

'Blessing for *what*?!'

'Blessing to go follow my dreams.'

7

AT No. 10 Henry Street Mrs Singh was putting out the rubbish, extra-large fleecy Minnie Mouse pyjamas shielding her from the winter chill.

Rising up behind, like an imperial fortress, Blackpool Football Club was the pride of the town, and the reason why houses on the short terraced row were so affordable. On match nights the house shook on its foundations, the windows rattling as if the end of the world had come.

Mrs Singh was about to slip back into the warm when she heard a voice.

'Mam.'

Turning, she looked fretfully out to the street.

'Hardeep!'

'Hello Mam.'

'Where have you been?!' she exclaimed, waving her youngest son to her.

'Just been to see Papa. Asked for his blessing. But he threw me out.'

'Oh-ho! Papa will come around.'

'Not this time, Mam. Says I've brought shame on the family. That I'm an effing disgrace.'

Harry's mum leaned in as her son approached. Embracing him, she kissed his cheeks, then the top of his head.

'Putting your turban back on would be a start.'

'A start to what?'

'To getting back in your Papa's good books.'

Harry grimaced.

'That's never gonna happen.'

'Course it will. His bark is worse than his bite.'

'He's the opposite of me, Mam. He worships money and rotting meat.'

'And Guru Nanak!' she added reproachfully.

'*And* Guru Nanak.' Harry sighed, pulling away from his mum's Minnie Mouse embrace. 'I'm not into any of that stuff, Mam. I'm a performer.'

'Oh-ho... your Maharaja!'

'I've retired him. He's gone. But I'd still rather work in the theatre than in selling dodgy meat to Paki restaurants.'

'No shame in business, love.'

'I know… but that's not what I'm interested in. Never have been. You know that.'

Mrs Singh dabbed a sleeve to her eye as if sobbing.

'Why not settle down like your brothers? They all have nice Punjabi girls. We'll find you one too. A pretty one!'

'Mam! I'm not going to settle down. Not gonna get hitched!'

'We'll find a girl and you can have a long engagement, that's all. Like paying the deposit on a house. Will be yours when you're ready to put the key in the lock.'

Harry Singh stepped back, his tongue streaked in the bitterest bile.

'I'm never gonna get married, Mam,' he said, the words spoken slow and loud. 'Not ever. I'm not interested in girls…'

'Course you are. All nice boys like girlies!'

'No, Mam. Not all. Some of us prefer men.'

8

TWO MUGS WERE slid fast down the vinyl tabletop at Mack's Café, waves of hot milky tea breaking over the sides.

Harry and Bitu sat in silence, each one too drained by life and misadventure to think of anything to say. When the mugs had been emptied, Harry leaned back in his chair, sighed, sneezed, and said:

'Pa threw me out. Says he won't take me back. I'm an

effing good-for-nothing. And, me Mam threw me out, too.'

'For being a good-for-nothing?'

Harry's expression dimmed, as if he'd seen death.

'Came out to her.'

'Bleedin'' 'eck!'

'Had to be done. Couldn't keep going on with the lie.'
Bitu grinned.

'So that's why I've never seen you with a girl!'

'You must have had your suspicions.'

'Thought it was 'cos you were a scaredy-cat.'
Bitu grinned again, wider than before. 'So Maharaja
Malipasse's a bleedin' poofter!'

'*Was*,' Harry corrected. 'He *was* a p… he was gay.'

Bitu winced.

'Have something to tell you, too.'

'What? Don't you dare friggin' tell me *you're* on my
team?'

'*Cah*! *No*! I love girls! They look pretty and they smell
nice.'

'Then?'

Digging a hand into the inside pocket of his donkey
jacket, Bitu fished out an official-looking envelope.

'This.'

'What is it?'

'They're sending me home.'

'But you *are* home.'

'They're sending me home to India.'

Harry frowned.

'They can't do that. You've been here thirty years. You've got residency!'

Bitu's eyes widened as if he was experiencing pain.

'Didn't quite do the paperwork,' he said.

'What? *Never*?!'

'Was busy. Busy working. Busy living.'

'So what's gonna happen?'

'They're bloody deporting me.'

'Christ! When?'

'Tomorrow,' Bitu said.

'What're you gonna do?'

'They're sending me to Delhi... paying for my ticket... on an aeroplane.'

'Course it's on an aeroplane! They're hardly gonna send you back by cruise ship!'

'Will go to the Kumbh Mela, the great spiritual gathering. Need to cleanse my bloody soul. I'll miss you,' Bitu mumbled, stuffing the letter away.

'Yeah, and me you, Bitu-bhai. We had some good times.'

Their focus trained on the chipped vinyl tabletop, Harry and Bitu lost themselves in the same chain of memories: one success after the next, and the run of ill-fortune... the Blackpool Grand debacle, the birthday party disaster, and walking away from the props at the end of the pier.

'You could go back and get the gear,' Bitu said. 'It'll

still be there.'

'Nah, it'll have been pinched by now… Anyway, I'm not going back. The Great Maharaja Malipasse is dead. Cremated on the magnificent funeral pyre of dead-end performers. I'm movin' on, not back!'

'On to what?'

'To… to… to a life of spontaneity… a life without the Curse of Harry Houdini!'

'Not that tripe again! All you do is go on about the Curse!'

'It's real, and you know it as well as me!'

'*Tosh*! That's what it is!'

'No it damn well isn't! Houdini and I share the same bloody name. And we both got the same bloody curse!'

Bitu regarded his friend with scorn.

'In case you've forgotten, Houdini's name was Ehrich… *Ehrich Weiss*. And you… you're not Harry either! You're bloody Hardeep Singh!'

Harry wasn't listening. His concentration had slipped back onto the tabletop's fake wood grain. As if cogs were spinning, he glowered, grinned, and exclaimed:

'I know how to break the curse, Bitu-bhai!'

'Oh god!'

'With magic!'

Bitu rolled his eyes.

'Magic just leads to trouble… you know that.'

'Not conjuring… not stage magic… *real* magic!'

'No such thing.'

'Course there is!' Harry cried, the café's regulars peering up from their red-tops. 'You just have to believe!'

'And where will you find the magic spell, the one to break the Curse of Mr Houdini?'

Harry's lungs swelled with air.

'In India of course!' he yelled.

9

AIR INDIA FLIGHT 543 touched down at New Delhi International on time, disgorging a flood of economy travellers into the terminal building.

Once the other passengers had disembarked, a clutch of deportees was chaperoned from the back of the aircraft to immigration. At least three of them were in tears, and two – an elderly couple from Leeds – had tied themselves to their seats, refusing to leave the aircraft.

Sorrowfully, Bitu Jain followed the stream of disgraced returnees to the immigration counter, where the accompanying British officer presented a stack of passports to her Indian counterpart.

Waiting his turn, Bitu was formally interviewed. His fingerprints taken, his passport was stamped and handed over to him.

'You are free to go,' the officer said.

Pacing through to the baggage hall, Bitu found Harry waiting.

'Smells like home,' he said.

'This is scary.'

'What is?'

'Coming to the country I'm from for the first time.'

'The whole world's from India,' Bitu said under his breath. 'But they just don't know it.'

10

WITH THEIR LUGGAGE in hand, the pair filed out into the sea of people, insects swarming over the floodlights outside.

As soon as they stepped through the automatic glass doors, throngs of taxi drivers and pimps rushed up, offering Harry their services.

'How do they know I'm a foreigner?'

'It's the smell you give off,' Bitu answered.

'That's nuts! I'm not giving off a smell.'

'Oh but you are Harry-bhai. You just don't know it.'

Five minutes later they'd been bustled into a groaning Ambassador taxi, the Sikh driver speeding into town, as though charging a steed into battle.

In a bid to take his mind off charging the spontaneous India trip to his credit card, Harry unwound the window, and pushed his face into the slipstream.

'Can't believe it!' he cried. 'I can't believe I'm here!'

Bitu gave a double thumbs up and wobbled his head. 'It's like I never left,' he said.

The taxi slalomed up to a no-frills hotel in Connaught Place, the gleaming white wheel of buildings built as the centrepiece of the Raj's capital.

They checked in and Bitu sloped straight off to bed.

As though called by a voice whispering to him, Harry hurried out through the doors and onto the street.

Excited to the pit of his stomach, he looked left, right, forward and back, up, down, his nostrils drawing in the scent of India for the first time.

Not the fake India of Manchester's Curry Mile, or the fragments of India you get at English market stalls – but Full Monty India, in dazzling 3D IMAX.

Everything Harry saw was fresh and, at the same time, he already knew it in a back-to-front way… as though he'd seen its reflection ten thousand times.

There were hawkers touting fake Rolexes, beggars selling *beedi* cigarettes, and street stalls offering *paan*, *jalebis* and fresh-squeezed juice. Although it was late, the streets were teeming with people – some moving forward briskly as if in a hurry, while others meandered slowly through the throng. More still paused to eat at one of the makeshift food stalls or to catch one of the many street performances.

At one, a troupe of young children were walking a tightrope slung between a pair of posts. Dressed in sequined costumes, they put on an acrobatic routine while breathing fire, as their older siblings played home-made instruments and begged for donations.

Pushing to the front, Harry was drawn in. He was captivated by the lack of safety, and by the fact there didn't seem to be anyone from the authorities in charge.

The under-age tightrope acrobats paused to spend their takings on rice and *daal*, while the audience sauntered away to the next street corner where another performance was getting underway.

Drifting over with the flow, Harry found himself at the front, a few feet from a slim sinewy figure in a scarlet knee-length cloak. Before him was a high trestle table, on which lay an ordinary wooden box, the size of a child's coffin.

A trumpet sounded in the background, hands clapped fast and hard, and the show began.

Declaring himself the greatest sorcerer in all India, the cloak-clad performer opened the box and pulled out a rabbit by the ears. On proving the creature was very much alive, he whipped a glass medicine bottle from his cloak. Prising open the rabbit's mouth, he poured a few drops of the mystery liquid onto its tongue.

The magician spun round and around three times.

By the time he stopped, the animal was dead.

The audience seemed displeased at the death of an innocent creature. As a wave of susurration coursed through the lines of onlookers, the magician did something unexpected. Unscrewing the top of the medicine bottle once again, he drank the poison, his face contorting.

The crowd gasped.

A drum rolled.

The sorcerer fell to the ground, as lifeless as the rabbit still clutched in his hand.

Again, the audience gasped and, again, the drum rolled.

A king-sized bed sheet was pulled over the casualties.

The magician's child rushed forward, shaking his dead father, begging him to come back to life.

The drum rolled a third time.

A young woman in the crowd began tearing out her hair. Unable to control herself, she begged the deities for a miracle.

A moment of despair passed.

Then the sheet twitched and jerked left and right, and the magician leapt to his feet.

In his hands was the rabbit – dazed but alive once again.

11

At breakfast next morning Harry sat in silence, replaying the magician's performance in his mind, while his friend sat across from him sipping his tea.

Since childhood he'd been enthralled by illusion, and by the way a stage magician diverts the audience's attention away from what's really going on. For Harry, one of the joys of stage magic was observing another performer's routine, and breaking it down point by point.

At once he saw through the trick:

The rabbit hadn't been poisoned, but rather had been strangled while the magician span round. Faking his own death, he'd substituted a live rabbit, which had been hidden in his cloak.

Bitu cleared his throat and sighed.

'So what is the programme?' he asked.

Harry hadn't heard, or if he had he wasn't interested in answering. His thoughts were still on the sorcerer.

'Harry-bhai!'

'Huh? What?'

'You've only been here two minutes and already you're zoned out.'

'Sorry. I was thinking about something.'

'About the Blackpool Grand?'

'No… I told you, The Great Maharaja Malipasse is dead.'

'So what's the programme?' Bitu repeated.

'To reinvent myself.'

'And get rid of the curse!'

'To reinvent myself and be free of the curse,' Harry said.

'Very good.'

'So… how d'you go about getting rid of a curse in India?'

'Immersion.'

'*Immersion*?'

'*Ha*, yes, immersion. That is right.'

'Immersion in what?'

'In a sacred river.'

'Which sacred river?'

'Ganga and Yamuna.'

'Both of them?'

'*Ha*, yes, both… at the *Sangam*.'

'What's that?'

'Where they meet together. It is extra-special blessed. Just looking at it removes all curses. But immersion in it gives even more blessing,' Bitu said.

'Where is it – the *Sangam*?'

'At Allahabad.'

'Where's that?'

'UP.'

'Uttar Pradesh?'

'*Ha*. We take the express train this afternoon.'

'What then?' Harry asked anxiously.

'Then we see what happens,' Bitu said.

12

LATE IN THE afternoon, the Poorva Express arrived at the station, iron wheels grinding and sparking against the tracks.

The station was packed to capacity, every available inch of space taken up by people, many with bundles on heads. Following close behind Bitu, Harry found himself breathless at the sheer number of people crammed onto the platform.

'Why are there so many people?!' he yelled.

'Kumbh Mela,' his friend called back.

'What's that?'

'Pilgrimage.'

Even before the train streamed into the station, the pilgrims did their damnedest to clamber aboard. Like a migrating species with no choice, they risked life and limb – the near-suicidal attempts to get inside causing injury and chaos.

Miraculously, Harry and Bitu managed to get on board, although forced to sit in the aisle of an overloaded carriage. Chattering and praying, the other passengers were whipped up with anticipation, as though about to take part in the single most important ceremony of their lives.

The locomotive jerked out from Delhi Station and through the miles of shantytown. Staring out the window, Harry watched the progression of life in horror.

The monumental buildings of the capital were quickly replaced by detritus. Women were scrubbing clothes in the sidings, their little children squatting nearby; rag-pickers and pye-dogs zigzagging through the undergrowth in search of scraps to stave off hunger.

Taking Bitu's advice, Harry had brought no more than a simple cloth bag, with a few knickknacks. Everything else was left at the hotel in the capital. Almost everyone else was travelling as light or even lighter – many of them dressed in single cotton sheets. Those who'd brought bundles along seemed to have packed little more than a few provisions and a rolled-up mattress.

Three hours outside Delhi, a tall blond foreigner pushed his way through into the carriage in which Harry and Bitu were squashed up on the floor. Unmistakably Canadian, he was wearing a backpack on which was sewn a large patch bearing his nation's flag. All kinds of stuff was dangling from the pack, including multiple water bottles, a sleeping bag, and a camping stove. The strap of a camera bag was furled around his wrist, and an iPhone hanging around his neck in a transparent pouch. Young and enthusiastic, he'd tapped into the general sense of elation, and was eager to share the experience with anyone who spoke English.

'Crazy, isn't it?!' he called out to Harry, picking up a sense that it was all new to him, too.

'Certainly is,' Harry retorted.

'Where are you guys from?' the Canadian asked.

'England. And you?'

'Toronto. I'm Marney... and you?'

'Harry... and this is Bitu.'

'Heading to the Kumbh?'

'Yeah.'

'First time?'

'Yeah.'

'Me too,' said Marney. 'I'm a Kumbh Mela virgin!'

The train stopped and what seemed like a hundred thousand people clambered on. So many pilgrims were compressed into the carriage that Harry relived the panic of being stuck in a locked coffin when a practice session went wrong.

'I'm not good with crowds,' he mumbled.

'Then I've got a feeling you're gonna find the Kumbh a challenge,' Marney replied.

'Lots of people there, are there?'

The Canadian rolled his eyes as Bitu wobbled his head from side to side.

'They're expecting a hundred million,' Marney said.

Harry looked at the foreigner as though he were stark raving mad.

'Impossible.'

'Nope, it's not.'

'What?!'

Harry shot Bitu a look of terror.

Again, Bitu wobbled his head from side to side.

'Give or take a few million,' he said.

13

AT THREE O'CLOCK next morning the train screeched into Allahabad Junction, the pilgrims twice as frantic to get off as they had been to get aboard.

Swept forward in a sea of people and scant possessions, Harry and Bitu were carried along by the tidal wave. Weighed down by his luggage, the Canadian was left behind, rooted to the spot.

Amid the pandemonium, hundreds of uniformed police armed with canes were doing what they could to keep the pilgrims in line. Three days earlier one of the station's pedestrian bridges had collapsed, killing dozens of devotees.

Unnerved by the sheer number of people, Harry did his best to calm himself. Half a pace ahead, Bitu led the way as though he knew exactly where he was going.

With no hope of catching an auto-rickshaw, let alone a taxi, they walked the final few miles to the pilgrimage point. As they did so, Harry's head buzzed with questions – the kind formulated by an Occidental mind. Having known Bitu for fifteen years, he knew full well that practical questions would have been met with indecisive answers, or yet more questions.

Once out of the railway station, the two friends reached the open road. Pressed all around them were tens of thousands of pilgrims. As in one of those scenes of mass human exodus that follow a natural disaster, they all had the same vacant expression. It was as though everyone was uncertain what the next minutes, let alone hours, would bring.

Shrouded in white and orange, the pilgrims resembled ghosts, their faces masked with expectation. In this stream of humanity, the old were carried on stretchers; the youngest on shoulders. Some families had tied a rope around themselves so that they didn't get separated in the throng. A number of people were crawling the route on their knees in grave danger of being sucked down in the maelstrom.

Surging forward, the stream of pilgrims began merging with other streams, gushing together from all directions. As the river expanded into a sea and then an ocean, it broke through onto the colossal floodplain of the Kumbh Mela itself.

As the first rays of dawn light broke over the horizon, Harry caught sight of the plateau, edged as it was by the Yamuna and the Ganga. Viewed from a distance it was like something from a Hollywood rendition of a Biblical tale – millions and millions of pilgrims filling the vast expanse.

Unnatural, and at the same time utterly natural, the scale defied description. The scene was tinged yellow by dawn, touched by some primordial alchemy.

Profoundly moved by the experience, Harry stopped dead still, the waves of pilgrims lapping past.

'Must keep going,' Bitu called. 'Not far to go now.'

'How often does this gathering take place?'

Bitu urged his friend to start moving again.

'Every twelve years,' he said. 'But every twelve-times-twelve years there's a big Mela… and this is it.'

Throwing his hands up above his head, Harry signalled to his friend.

'What?!'

'Every one hundred and forty-four years,' said Bitu, making the calculation.

'I don't believe it!' Harry bellowed. 'You're telling me the biggest Kumbh Mela in my lifetime happens to be taking place just when we turned up?'

Bitu wobbled his head in agreement.

'Yes, like that.'

'But that's impossible! It can't just happen now – when I needed it to get rid of the curse.'

Bitu Jain frowned at his friend, pulling him to move faster.

'Nothing is impossible in India,' he said.

14

FOR THREE DAYS and nights, Harry followed the routine of every other pilgrim.

At the appointed times he strode down to the isthmus between the Ganga and the Yamuna, venturing there in the wake of the charging naked *naga* holy men. Immersing himself in the water, with literally millions of others around him, he felt as though he were part of something far greater than he'd ever experienced before.

Stripped naked and being cleansed by the hallowed water, the pilgrims seemed oblivious of the commotion around them. As far as they were concerned, they were alone – bound by a sacred bond to the pantheon and ritual of the Hindu faith.

Having immersed himself four times, purifying his soul and dispelling the curse, Harry left Bitu at the ramshackle tent where they were staying, and roamed through the hordes of disciples.

Dozens of pontoon bridges spanned the waterways, each one of them packed with pilgrims. The plateau itself had been laid with great sheets of steel so as to prevent the faithful from being sucked down into the mud.

Skirting around the individual clusters of humanity, hailing from all corners of India, Harry made his way to a lip of higher ground. Every few feet there was a stall selling hot cooked food or such things as flower garlands, clothing, devotional banners, fluorescent pink candy-floss and bottled drinks. In the background constant announcements for lost children blared out over loudspeakers.

Away from the general hullabaloo, Harry reached a far more tranquil area, its expanse dotted with simple white canvas tents. Seated or standing before each was a huddle of figures. In each case, one person was being fussed over or lauded, while devotees streamed up, hoping to be blessed.

Outside one canopy a godman was sitting cross-legged. Seemingly ancient, he was holding his left arm up in the air. The limb was wizened and gnarled; he hadn't allowed it to fall for thirty-three years. At another tent, a holy man was standing on one foot, as he had supposedly done in complete silence since 1971.

Harry was about to retrace his steps to where he and Bitu were staying, when something caught his eye. Against a setting of oddity and wonder, it stuck out not because it was astonishing, but rather on account of its familiarity.

Surrounded by a knot of devotees, a young *sadhu* dressed in a simple lungi and turban was lying outstretched on a bed of nails beside a campfire. To the delight of the pilgrims, he stood up and followed the feat with another.

His palms pressed together under his chin, he mumbled a mantra faster and faster. Then, with the audience pressing forward, he rubbed thumb and forefinger of either hand together, his eyes still closed.

To the amazement of those gathered around, his hands began to stream with oyster-grey smoke.

Lids lifting from his eyes, he said something in Hindi, at which one of the disciples lurched forward, grasped his wrist and felt for his pulse.

Her face rapt in consternation, the pilgrim exclaimed in the negative – there wasn't one. Any normal human without a pulse would be dead – but the *sadhu* was evidently anything but normal.

Intrigued, Harry stepped forward, joining the crowd of devotees. He watched as the *sadhu* picked a dagger from the ground and ran the blade over his thigh. Steel brushing over skin, it left a trail of crimson blood – at which the holy man's minions gasped in anguish and delight.

Wiping away the blood, the ascetic showed that the wound had miraculously healed. Then, without wasting a moment, he held the dagger's blade in the campfire until it glowed orange. Pulling it out, he swigged from a tin cup of sacred water, spat, and touched the red-hot blade to his tongue.

As the disciples cooed and gasped, Harry walked

round to the side of the group, and stood a distance behind the *sadhu*. Unobserved, he watched as a variety of other miraculous feats were executed.

First, the godman sprinkled *vibhuti*, holy ash, onto the palms of the audience. Next, he pierced a fold of flesh at his waist with a meat skewer. After that, he prayed and it appeared to rain – a few drops at least.

Having seen enough, Harry zigzagged back towards the filthy tent where Bitu was waiting for him. Although the ground was veiled in thick steel sheets, almost everyone was spattered with mud. But no one seemed to care in the least. Being present at the Kumbh Mela was to be set apart from the tribulations of daily life – and to be blessed in a deep down way.

In a bid to avoid the arterial stream of pilgrims heading towards him, Harry ventured to the plateau's eastern flank and found himself in an area he hadn't visited before.

Fenced off, it was well-drained and exceptionally clean. There was none of the litter or the mess found in the main public zone. Immaculately dressed in pure white robes with white crocheted beanie hats, the pilgrims residing there were spotlessly clean. Unlike everyone else Harry had seen at the Kumbh, they were a vision of order and sterility – each of them with a bottle of cleansing gel hanging around their necks with strings of prayer beads.

The other difference between the white-garbed

devotees and all the other pilgrims, was that they weren't Indian, but foreigners. Pacing through the pristine encampment, Harry heard English, French, German, Spanish, and Chinese spoken. As he wondered who they all were and what was going on, someone called his name.

He turned.

The Canadian from the train rushed up.

'Come for the *darshan*?' he asked energetically.

'Huh?'

'The *darshan*. It's about to start.'

'What *darshan*?'

'The one Mother Mee holds every evening. You are here for Mother Mee, aren't you?' Marney uttered severely.

'Um, er… yes… That's right. Yes, I'm here for Mother Mee.'

'Fantastic! I'll show you where it is!'

Harry wanted to ask who Mother Mee was, but feared doing so would single him out as an outsider. So he went along with it and found himself cross-legged on the ground inside a large hexagonal marquee. Everyone else was dressed in spotless white – all of them foreigners, and all with their gaze trained on the dais at the front.

'Any minute now,' Marney whispered in a tense voice.

'Great,' said Harry.

A droning noise of unbridled anticipation began in the front row and moved progressively backwards. Like the sound of an insect colony, it made no sense to anyone unconnected with the group.

A minute or two passed in which a team of technicians hurried about testing the PA system. Amid rapturous applause, Mother Mee stepped into the blinding white light of the stage.

Her delicate bare feet on ivory-white petals, she seemed to float effortlessly from the wings and into the centre of the dais.

Palms pressed together in greeting, the female *sadhu* dipped her head towards the audience in deference. Furled in white robes and crocheted beanie like her multitude of followers, she was blessed with an ear-to-ear grin, and a sense of utter tranquillity.

Harry's gaze followed her, as he observed how the beams of two powerful spotlights glided along with her. Once seated, the godwoman sat silently in prayer for a few minutes, as though taking her time. Closing their eyes, the pilgrims prayed, clearing their minds in preparation of the sermon that was to come.

Slipping on a wireless headset, Mother Mee thanked the deities, recited a short invocation, and began to address her followers. Although Indian, her accent was imbued with a mid-Atlantic twang, as though she'd spent many years abroad. Speaking slowly, she talked about pure love and pure joy – the kind untainted by the shortcomings of mankind.

For the two and a half hours Mother Mee spoke, the

pilgrims listened. Among them, Harry yearned to get up and leave – but doing so would have caused him to stand out. So he sat there, his crossed legs aching and numb, his back sorer than sore.

To his left, Marney the Canadian seemed to glow as if bathed in supreme and unconditional love. His ears drank up the oration, his eyes ingesting the scene of fantastical white.

When it was over, Mother Mee stood up, blew kisses to the audience, and glided off in the same way she'd arrived. Even though she had left, the devotees didn't move. Lost in a state of reflective meditation, they hung on for a long while, before drifting away in ones and twos.

Long after dark, Harry slunk back to the tent, where he found Bitu stretched out on a *charpoy*.

'I've seen wonders,' he said.

'Wonderful girls… or were they wonderful *boys*?!'

'Not girls or boys. Wonderful godmen, and godwomen, too.'

'*Sadhus*?'

Harry nodded.

'I'll take you to see them tomorrow,' he said.

Bitu clicked his tongue, signalling a lack of interest.

'No time for godmen,' he spat. 'They're all tricksters and fakes.'

'Doesn't mean they're not interesting,' Harry replied. 'I saw one out there this afternoon passing off stage magic as real miracles!'

'Told you, they're tricksters and fakes – and they're doing rubbish!'

Harry stared into space, his attention straying.

'It wasn't rubbish,' he countered softly. 'The young guy was performing high-level stuff. Just don't understand where he got the chemicals.'

'*Chemicals*?'

'The ones needed for the tricks.'

Again, Bitu clicked his tongue.

'This is India!' he yelled. 'You can get anything you like!'

'Even insanely dangerous chemicals?'

'Especially insanely dangerous chemicals!' cried Bitu.

15

THE MORNING AFTER Mother Mee's *darshan*, Harry left Bitu sleeping on his *charpoy* and strolled to the confluence of the two sacred rivers.

Wending his way between the rows of tents, and the streams of pilgrims, he thought how amazing it was that life at the greatest human gathering in history now seemed somehow normal. Harry may have only been in India for a handful of days, but he felt at home there. The layers of life were set apart from the grim, hollow realities of Blackpool.

Down at the shore pilgrims were immersing themselves, each one lost in silent ritual. For most it was the journey of a lifetime, having ventured from distant parts of India. Yet more had come from abroad – from Europe, Africa, the Americas and beyond.

The dark surface of the water was touched by the first strains of yellow light, as though an enchanted cloak had been cast over the scene. At that moment, standing at the river's margin, Harry knew his life would never be quite the same again.

It wasn't a case of conversion – he'd never been a believer, even though his family assumed he was a devout Sikh like the rest of them. The sheer numbers of devotees had touched Harry in a non-spiritual way – as though every one of them was linked to him through raw humanity.

As the sun's golden light swathed the bathers, the water rippled and churned by the activity, Harry watched a family make their way gingerly to the shore.

A thick blue cord was strung around the huddle, keeping the little group safely together. There must have been fifteen of them spanning four or even five generations – from newborn babes in arms to toothless crones. The women's ankles were fettered with heavy silver bands, the kind worn in the remote landscape of Arunachal Pradesh, from where they had come.

Keeping in formation, they slipped into the water, immersing themselves all together.

Awed, Harry gave thanks to the forces of nature for allowing him to have witnessed such an event. Once

again he marvelled how the supreme Maha Kumbh
Mela – held once every century and a half – was taking
place just when he needed it. The coincidence seemed
too much – as if it wasn't a coincidence at all.

For a moment, Harry found himself wondering
whether he'd been lured to the land of his ancestors by a
higher calling. *Nonsense*, he thought to himself, strolling
back towards the tent. Thinking like that was the first
step on a ladder leading to madness.

16

BITU WAS STRETCHED out on the rope bed, picking his
teeth with the end of a *neem* stick.

'Got something for you,' he said as Harry approached.

'What?'

Bitu clicked his tongue, angling the sound towards
the space under where he was lying.

'Take it out.'

'Huh?'

'Look under the *charpoy*!'

Harry stooped down and removed a damp cardboard
box filled with an assortment of bottles and dented metal
tins.

'What's all this?'

'Left by a *sadhu*, that's what.'

'Left where?'

'Here… the tent's owner gave it to me – said it was a
hazard to life and limb.'

Perching on the edge of the *charpoy*, Harry looked through the box, reading the labels, his forehead furrowing.

'Sulphuric acid, sulpho-cyanide, ferric chloride… *Jesus*! This is as dangerous as it gets! They're the kind of chemicals Houdini used to do his tricks – it's stuff that's hard to come by in England unless you've got a licence.'

'In India there's no such problem with paperwork,' retorted his friend.

'No need for doctors' prescriptions?'

Bitu-bhai let out a cackle, then coughed.

'Of course not! That's why India's so much fun!'

As the sentence was spoken, the heavens opened and a torrential downpour began. Out on the plain, drenched pilgrims staggered about packing and repacking their belongings.

'Hate rain!' cried Bitu, stretched out on the bed.

'I'm sure it'll end in a minute,' Harry chipped in.

Three hours later there was still no sign of a respite. Racing in from the west, a fresh crop of storm clouds emptied their contents over the Kumbh Mela, along with lightning and hail.

Bored out of his mind, Harry looked through the box again, scribbling notes on a scrap of paper. Grunting from time to time, his spirits seemed buoyed.

Late in the afternoon the storm moved on and the rain stopped as though a leak had been fixed in the sky.

'We'd better think about getting back to Delhi,'

said Bitu, sitting up. 'With rain like that the trains'll be delayed.'

Harry looked at his friend and smiled.

'Got an idea,' he said.

Bitu narrowed his eyes.

'No time for nonsense!'

Clapping his hands, Harry dragged his friend up from the *charpoy*, grabbed the cardboard box, and led the way outside.

Ten minutes later, Harry was attired in a *salwar kameez*, a voluminous turban on his head in the same shade of saffron. Having picked up a couple of props, he gave the signal.

'You sure you want to do this?' barked Bitu gruffly.

'Yes! It'll cheer everyone up.'

'But you said Maharaja Malipasse is dead.'

'Then I won't be Malipasse.'

'So who shall I say's about to perform?'

Harry glanced left, then right – taking in the sea of rubbish stirred up by the storm. His eyes stopped on an empty plastic packet of soap powder. Blue and red printed on white, it bore the logo of the OMO brand.

'*Omo-ji*,' said Harry.

'Sounds stupid.'

'What does it matter? I told you, it's just for fun!'

17

GROANING, BITU THRUST up his arms, announcing that

The Great Omo-ji had arrived from a land beyond the horizon.

No one seemed to care – they had far more pressing matters to think about than watching a magic act. Sorting out their drenched belongings was the only thing on their minds.

'They're not interested!' Bitu spat. 'Let's go back inside where it's warm.'

Undeterred, Harry pushed the headdress down tight on his head and began.

For his first trick, he took a hundred-rupee note from his pocket, held it up for all to see, and set fire to it.

But the money didn't burn.

Although it passed off perfectly, the trick was witnessed by a single devotee, and only because he was lame, and was resting for a moment before carrying on.

For his second trick, The Great Omo-ji smashed a coconut on the steel sheet beneath his feet. Erupting in fire, the white meat inside was drenched red as though filled with blood.

The explosion secured Harry three more spectators.

Moving swiftly on, he stopped his pulse, as the magician in Delhi had done. Then, in a pièce de résistance, he flicked open his fist, causing a fireball to billow out from nowhere.

Bemused, the audience sloped away.

'That was fun!' Harry exclaimed with delight. 'Can't say it was a full house, but it was good to perform.'

Bitu was unimpressed – not with the magic, but with his friend.

'That was a waste of time!' he snapped.

18

THAT EVENING HARRY and Bitu sat on their *charpoys*, considering what to do next.

'I'll go to Meerut,' said Bitu.

'To your family?'

'*Ha*. They'll wonder where I've been.'

'Where you've been since we landed in Delhi?'

Bitu shook his head melancholically.

'Where I've been for the last thirty-two years,' he said.

'You mean you never told them you were in England?!'

Wobbling his head, Bitu indicated the negative.

'No,' he said after a long pause.

'Why not?!'

'I never got round to it.'

Harry pushed a hand back through his hair.

'I never asked you why you went to England in the first place.'

'*Why*? They married me off. That's why!'

Harry balked at the news.

'What about your wife? Did she go with you?'

'No. She stayed at Meerut. No money for two tickets.'

'But she knows you went to England, right?'

Again, Bitu's head wobbled.

'Not exactly. She thinking I went to Bombay.'

'And I thought *I* was a screw-up!' Harry bellowed.

Mulling over their troubles, each was lost in his own state of self-imposed misery.

'Now we're cleansed, what to do?' Bitu asked. 'Home to Blackpool?'

'Back to the grey and the cold?' Harry answered, the words pained.

'I love that place.'

'Well I don't. Hate the idea of getting a job… a *real* job… chopping up bones for minimum wage.'

'You could stay in India,' Bitu offered.

'And do what?'

'Magic tricks?'

Harry scoffed at the idea.

'Told you, I'm done with all that. Anyway, you saw for yourself – it went down like a lead balloon.'

Sitting up, Bitu dug the end of a finger into his right ear, coughed hard, and cleared his throat.

'On my travels I've learnt one thing,' he said.

'What?'

'That if you relax, the path opens up.'

Harry looked round at his friend.

'You're sounding like a bleedin' godman.'

'No chance of that!' Bitu said.

After much deliberating, the pair decided to take the train back to Delhi, collect their luggage from the hotel in Connaught Place, and to follow their chosen paths.

Next morning, Harry braved the pit-latrine, and found himself wishing he was a thousand miles away from the Kumbh Mela. It may have been the greatest gathering in human history, but it was short on creature comforts.

Trudging back from the toilet, he found Bitu charging about hysterically.

'It's gone! It's gone!' he cried.

'What has?'

'My money and passport!'

Grabbing the knot of dirty laundry he was using as a pillow, Harry searched for his own valuables.

'*Jesus Christ!*' he yelled. 'They got me as well!'

'I hate this country!' Bitu whimpered. 'Wish I could go home.'

'This *is* your home!' Harry growled scathingly.

Collapsing on their *charpoys*, they sat in silence, wondering what to do. One by one they crossed off all possibilities in their heads.

'We're outcasts,' Bitu said.

'So what do we do – *beg*?'

'This isn't Blackpool! Who's gonna give us money?'

'We could go to a soup kitchen. There's one over where the *sadhus* hang out. Saw loads of pilgrims getting fed for free there yesterday.'

'A bowl of soup is one thing,' Bitu countered, 'but money and passport's another.'

'You mean we're gonna be stuck here at the Kumbh Mela forever?'

'In three weeks everyone will have gone and the waters will roll back with the new moon.'

'So, we're stuffed, right?' Harry muttered.

His friend didn't reply. He just sat on his *charpoy* staring into space.

After what seemed like an age, Bitu looked round.

'The Great Omo-ji can save us,' he said.

Harry mumbled an insult.

'Listen to me,' Bitu said, reaching over and tugging his friend's sleeve.

'*Bitu-bhai*! You saw how the tricks went down. No one took any notice.'

'And why not?'

'Because they've got other stuff on their minds.'

'No, no, no,' Bitu shot back. 'Not that.'

'Then, you tell me why no one watched the magic tricks – I did them well enough.'

'Very simple reason,' Bitu said. 'You did them as a stage magician.'

'What's wrong with that?'

'Should have performed them as a godman,' Bitu said.

PART II

1

As though getting ready for a show at the Blackpool Grand, Harry and Bitu devoted three full days to meticulous preparation.

Planning an entirely new routine from scratch, they put together a variety of rudimentary props discarded by the pilgrims out on the plain.

Although agnostic, Harry was superstitious – which partly explained why he'd come to the subcontinent to rid himself of Houdini's curse. In his mind, superstition was not related to religion, but was rather connected to tribulations hounding those involved in the performing arts.

Contravening the laws of his ancestral faith, by imitating a holy man, caused him no anguish at all. But doing so breached his superstitious mindset. Fearful at landing himself with a new curse, having been so recently cleansed of the last, he voiced his concerns.

Bitu swished a hand angrily through the air.

'We're just getting a little travelling money to get back to Delhi!' he exclaimed.

'Then why're we bothering to set it up as we are?'

'This is the Kumbh Mela!' Bitu cried. 'Godmen are two a penny out there. If it's not perfect, no one will notice you.'

Harry rolled his eyes.

'All right. But it's only one show – *agreed*?'

'One performance, *ha*, yes… except…'

'Except what?'

'Except if it's a resounding success, we could book extra performances.'

'*No!*' Harry yelled. 'One performance and that's all. An hour and a half and not a minute more.'

Wobbling his head in agreement, Bitu cleared his throat.

'All right,' he said. 'But it seems like a shame not to give people more if that's what they want.'

Harry wasn't listening.

'There's a problem,' he said.

'What's the matter Harry-bhai?'

'If we're passing the performance off as real magic, how'll we make money?'

'What d'you mean?'

Harry looked at his friend.

'At the Blackpool Grand people buy tickets, and at a street performance there's a tin cup.'

'*So?*'

'So how do we get people to donate to The Great Omo-ji?'

'Leave that to me,' said Bitu.

2

THAT EVENING, WHILE Harry practised his routine, his friend slipped out of the tent, his shadow roaming over miles of canvas.

Every square inch of space was taken up with tents, stalls, prayer circles, and people – all woven together in a mesmerizing tapestry of devotion. Clusters of pilgrims huddled in the darkness, ringing hand bells and singing mantras. Peppered about between their groups were naked *sadhus* – some chanting, others drawing on their *chilam* pipes.

Hurrying past, Bitu followed the directions he'd been given by an official at the Lost & Found office. Unlike Harry, he wasn't in the least superstitious, and had no interest at all in religion. Through his childhood in Meerut, he'd been tormented by *pundits* and *pujas*, and by a maternal grandmother who forced him to pray morning and night.

After forty minutes of scurrying in zigzag, he reached the rock bluff at the edge of the plateau. Following the ant-like stream of devotees trailing up, he clambered to the top.

Days and nights spent down on the plain had given Bitu a sense of the Kumbh Mela, as seen from the inside out. Viewing it as he now was from a considerable height provided a completely different perspective. The plateau was humming, the tents, pilgrims, the Yamuna and the Ganges swathed in eerie yellow floodlights.

Holding stock-still, Bitu observed it more keenly than anything he'd ever watched before. Despite the distance and the darkness, it was as if his mind mapped every single camp, food stall, block of pit-latrines, and silhouette.

Inhaling, he rubbed his eyes, cursed to himself, got

his story straight, and strode purposefully into The Imperial – a luxurious private tented encampment reserved for well-heeled travellers.

Waylaying a guard at the door he slipped him a folded message, declaring it was for the urgent attention of the Maharaja of Patiala.

The guard hurried away, the note in his hand.

Heading in the opposite direction, Bitu slipped into the magnificent tented salon. Radiating confidence as though he owned the place, he sat down on a cane planter's chair.

In recent years, Bitu Jain may have assumed the role of a magician's attendant, but his training was as an impersonator. What had begun as an amusement at school, had become a trade. Married off to a woman he'd not met until the day of the wedding, Bitu had blown his wife's dowry on a one-way ticket to Manchester, and on setting himself up for the stage.

After fifteen years of success and failure, he'd met Harry Singh. Unlike him, the young illusionist was brimming with enthusiasm. Without planning it, the course of their lives ran along the same path.

In his heyday, Bitu had prided himself on being able to mimic almost any accent, specializing in the inflections and mannerisms of the upper crust.

Casting an eye across the salon disparagingly, he gave the appearance of being revolted rather than impressed. All the guests appeared very wealthy, and most were foreigners – uniformly dressed in the attire of spiritual devotees. Across from him was a party of Americans from Tennessee. Sharing stories of the pilgrimage, they took it in turns to gush about everything and everyone they'd seen.

Ready for the performance, Bitu counted backwards from ten.

Three… two… one…

Right on cue, a white-gloved concierge stepped into the tented salon, a small brass bell in one hand and a folded note in the other.

'Message for His Highness the Maharaja of Patiala!' he cried, as the bell chimed. 'Message for the Maharaja of Patiala!'

On hearing the name, the Americans broke off from their conversation and peered around, eager to know who the member of royalty could be. Taking his time, Bitu signalled as discreetly as he was able. The message was borne over to him at speed. Giving thanks, he took it, pretended to read it, and slipped it away.

As soon as the concierge departed, one of the Americans approached.

'Excuse me Your Highness,' he intoned, subservience in his voice, 'I couldn't help but overhear you are the Maharaja of…'

'Of *Patiala.*'

Bowing reverently, the American glowed with honour and delight.

'I'm Rosco Schultz,' he said, reaching forward. Rather than offering his hand to be shaken, Bitu held it out, the knuckles facing upwards.

Taking the cue, Rosco from Tennessee kissed the back of the Maharaja's hand.

News of the distinguished guest's presence spread like wildfire.

Within ten minutes of his knuckles being kissed, he'd been introduced to all thirty members of the American party, comprised of Rosco's family and friends. Each one appeared more well-heeled than the last. Among them were shipping magnates Fred and Marsha Havilland, an heiress named Elaine Frogmore, and celebrated philanthropist, Felicity Frosch. Rushing from their tents at double-speed, they cooed over the member of royalty – who played the part as though his life depended on it.

Offered fresh mango juice and canapés, the Maharaja of Patiala waved it all aside, having assumed the guise of a troubled man.

'Forgive me but I cannot take refreshments at this difficult time,' he said, the Americans hanging on every word.

Concerned, they enquired what was the matter. The ruler waved the questions away as he had done the canapés.

'Forgive me, but it would be indiscreet to speak of the matter,' he said.

Her eyes welling with tears, one of the women lowered

her head and pleaded. At witnessing such a sincere and heartfelt request for information, the Maharaja of Patiala lifted the veil on his woes.

With the Americans clustered around he explained how, three years before, the palace vaults had been burgled, and how his people had been reduced to lives poverty. Blow by blow, he detailed how the chief of police had been behind the robbery. As the theft took place he, the rightful Maharaja of Patiala, was discredited as a fraud.

Having been arrested and chained, he was accused of drug dealing. Stripped of his ancestral wealth, the chief of police seized the palace, and even the Maybach presented to his grandfather by Adolf Hitler back in 1935.

'That's truly terrible!' one of the ladies exclaimed, holding a hand to her face.

'It's been an awful time,' Bitu said coldly, his voice a hybrid of aristocratic accents honed on the playing fields of Eton, and in the halls of the Moti Bagh Palace of Patiala.

A tall man at the back asked the Maharaja whether he'd regained his property. It was exactly the question Bitu had been waiting for.

Closing his eyes in a moment of mute reflection, he breathed in, his lungs filling to capacity.

'Thankfully, I'm blessed,' he said. 'Blessed to have loyal subjects, a loving family and, above all else, blessed to have a spiritual master unlike any other. He's the reason I am at the Kumbh Mela. While I stay up here in the lap of luxury, he resides down on the plain, living as a humble pilgrim. However hard I begged him to join me here, he adamantly refused. I feel wretched of course, that the greatest spiritual master in all of India should be down there with the ordinary people.'

Thirty mouths spat out the same question:

'What's the guru's name?'

Eyes welling with tears of devotion, the Maharaja of Patiala swallowed:

'His name is Sri Omo-ji,' he said.

3

As HE SLEPT that night, Harry relived the terror of a recurring nightmare at the Blackpool Grand – the casket jammed shut and the audience baying for his blood.

Drenched in sweat, he lay on the *charpoy*, the sound of a pilgrim reciting prayers in the next tent. At dawn, Bitu shook his friend's arm.

'Wakey wakey!'

Harry sat up, his expression downcast.

'I'm not doing it,' he said.

'Course you are!'

'No… it's not right. It's not what the Kumbh is about.'

Bitu clicked his knuckles, then cracked his neck.

'Just one show,' he uttered caringly. 'Then you're done.'

'That's not the point,' Harry said.

'If you feel so high and mighty,' his friend replied,

'why don't you give half the money to good causes?'

'What's the point?'

'You'll be helping others while you help yourself.'

Sighing like a man sentenced to the gallows, Harry dipped his head in a nod.

'All right. We'll do that – we'll give half the money to good causes… and whatever happens we'll do one performance and no more!'

Bitu wobbled his head.

'Let's get you ready,' he said.

4

AT NINE O'CLOCK, Omo-ji stepped from the tent, he and his single devotee having gone over every detail of the act.

Although similar in some ways, a stage show was quite different from the routine of a godman performing what was being passed off as real magic. As Harry strode out to the spot they'd chosen the day before, he was weighed down with worry.

'This is fraud!' he snapped, his bare feet pacing over the steel sheets paving much of the plateau.

'Stop thinking that!' Bitu growled.

'I can't! This is the Kumbh Mela – the one place on Earth where you're supposed to behave yourself!'

Stuffing a blanket into the box of chemicals and props on his head, Bitu turned.

'Don't be stupid!' he yelled. 'You think any of the *sadhus* here are doing real magic – you saw right through their acts as quickly as I did.'

'But doing this, I'm lowering myself to their level.'

Bitu snarled, the muscles of his face taut with ire.

'We're doing it because we've been robbed! So let's get on with it and we'll be on the first train out tonight!'

'What happens if no one turns up?'

'Do the routine exactly as we've planned it, and I promise you they will,' Bitu said.

At the selected spot, Bitu put the box down, laid out the woollen blanket, and weighted the edges with pebbles.

'Look at this – it's hexagonal!' Harry snapped. 'Couldn't you have got a square one like everyone else?'

'It's all I could find!' Bitu answered. 'And anyway, you're not like everyone else! Get into character and don't get out of it until I give you a sign we're done!'

Huffing and puffing, Harry stepped into the middle of the blanket, sat down cross-legged, and closed his eyes. Once his master was in position, Bitu covered the box with an old shirt, and double-checked they could be seen from the path leading up to the Imperial Camp.

'How long do I have to sit here like this?!' Harry whispered from the corner of his mouth. 'My legs are killing me!'

'Don't move till I tell you!' Bitu hissed.

Taking his place at the margin where the hexagonal blanket ended and the metal sheet began, he dipped his head in prayer, palms pressed together in line with his nose.

All around, the throngs of devotees got on with their own routines – doing their ablutions, praying, and strolling down to the water to immerse themselves.

Harry was about to complain yet again, and call the whole thing off, when a shrill American voice called out from the distance:

'Your Highness!'

5

APPROACHING REVERENTLY, THE thirty Americans from Tennessee washed forwards like a wave breaking over rocks, their eyes bright with wonder, and their teeth bared in ear-to-ear grins.

Bitu shot to his feet, his mind firmly trained on being the Maharaja of Patiala.

'So pleased you came,' he intoned in the aristocratic voice of his avatar.

'Your Highness, it's an honour!' exclaimed Rosco, ushering the others forward.

One by one the Americans lined up to kiss the royal hand, while the Maharaja begged them to stop. No more than a few feet away, Harry opened an eye and tried to make sense of what was going on.

Having greeted the aristocrat, the Americans ducked their heads subserviently once again, remembering they were not only with royalty but also in the presence of a living god.

'He's so handsome!' one of the ladies cooed.

'Simply divine!' cried another.

'This is so special,' whispered a third.

Rosco, who'd taken on the role as the group's leader, turned to the Maharaja.

'Your Highness,' he said, 'would it be asking too much to sit here for a few minutes, and join you in prayer?'

'Nothing would please His Celestial Highness more,' Bitu said.

Gasping at the honour, the Americans sat down beside the Maharaja, the godman seated in silence a few feet away from him.

After ten minutes of hushed invocation, Sri Omo-ji opened his eyes. His gaze focused on the middle distance, he was rigid in a trance-like state of meditation.

The Maharaja leant over to Rosco.

'He's waking from his journey,' he whispered.

The information was quickly passed from mouth to ear, until all thirty of the Americans had heard it.

Then, with sixty-two eyes trained on him, Omo-ji opened his mouth, plucked a pearl from his tongue, and placed it on the woollen blanket.

'What's that?' Rosco queried.

'A Dreamseed,' the Maharaja said. 'It's a sacred object – a miracle of miracles... an emblem of peace and love!'

Again, the information was whispered from one to the next, as the sense of awe swelled, and as Harry's legs went completely numb.

Reaching forwards, Bitu picked the pearl from the

blanket, and passed it to Rosco.

'For you.'

'Oh my, oh my! What an honour!' the American declared, as his friends bristled with jealousy.

Omo-ji plucked a second Dreamseed from his tongue. Although on best behaviour, the foreigners drooled at the thought of having such a venerated token of peace and love.

Bitu picked the pearl from the blanket, kissed it, and passed it to an elderly lady on his right.

'May it bring you inner joy,' he whispered.

Fawning, the woman took the seed on her palm, her face a vision of ecstasy.

A light breeze broke over the plain. As it faded, Omo-ji emitted a guttural humming noise from the base of his throat. A cross between the sound of someone being strangled and pure, unfettered pain, it ended as unexpectedly as it had begun.

'What's happening?' Rosco asked in a forced whisper.

'"The Calling",' the Maharaja of Patiala responded.

'What's that?'

'His Celestial Highness is about to speak.'

Urgently, Rosco relayed the news to the woman beside him, and she passed it on.

A surge of anticipation tore through the group.

Clenching his right hand into a fist, the godman blew on it as if extinguishing a candle's flame. Watching in awe, the Americans wondered what the guru was going to say.

'Truth is love and love is wisdom,' Omo-ji concluded in a hushed tone. 'Wisdom is truth, and hope is the radiance of the stars.'

'That's so lovely,' Rosco mumbled.

'So profound,' another said.

'It's called the "Mantra of Union",' Bitu explained, making it up as he went along. 'The words we speak first thing in the morning and last thing at night – when we are lonely or sad, and in times of fear.'

Together, the American devotees repeated the Mantra of Union:

'Truth is love and love is wisdom. Wisdom is truth, and hope is the radiance of the stars.'

'We repeat it thirty-one times, as there are thirty-one of us,' the Maharaja of Patiala explained.

Accordingly, the devotees from Tennessee spoke the mantra over and over until the phrase flowed effortlessly from their mouths.

When they'd finished, Omoji broke into gibberish:

'*Barak no hapak jil mos lu fan ti ga.*'

His hand clutching the Dreamseed, Rosco shrugged. 'What's he saying?'

'He's speaking the Language of the Crystal Heavens,' Bitu elucidated. 'It's an announcement – a signal, that the miracles will begin.'

His legs numb with pins and needles, Omo-ji stood, his eyes still trained on the middle distance.

'What's he gonna do now?' someone whispered, as another breeze coursed over the plain.

'The first miracle,' the Maharaja said.

Grasping a coconut from the edge of the blanket, the godman stepped over to the steel sheet beyond it and threw it down hard. As soon as the nut split open, it hissed, then erupted in fire.

The Americans gasped in amazement.

'This fire is a symbol of the purest love and passion,' said Bitu. 'The kind that echoes the deeds of humanity, and blesses from outside in.'

As the Americans absorbed the information, a second miracle was performed.

Still standing, Omo-ji removed a knife from the folds of his turban and drew the blade in a zigzag line down his arm, the wound glistening with fresh blood.

'No!' one of the Americans cried. 'Don't let him hurt himself!'

'Omo-ji feels no pain,' Bitu answered. 'He is not among us but on his own spiritual plane.'

For the third miracle, the godman rubbed both hands over his face, blinked three times, and began to choke.

'Is he OK?' asked Rosco fast.

'It is "the Reckoning",' the Maharaja said.

'What do you mean?'

'Watch,' said Bitu.

Eyes trained on the holy man, the Americans witnessed as Omo-ji's choking turned to retching.

Alarmed, they all had the same thought – that he was gravely unwell.

As they watched, the guru's lips parted and a fragment of shiny black could be seen. Taking it in his fingers, Omo-ji pulled. Little by little the object was revealed. An inch-thick strand of what looked like rubber, it ran to the height of a man, and glistened in the bright winter light.

'What is it?' the man sitting beside Rosco asked.

'We call it *asheervaad*,' Bitu answered. 'The "blessing".'

Apparently exhausted by the miracle, the godman shook his hands three times, before sitting on the hexagonal blanket once again. Then, clenching his right hand into a fist, he rubbed thumb and forefinger together causing white ash to stream down.

'*Look*!' one of the women cried.

'Oh my goodness!' wailed another.

'A miracle!' wheezed a third.

The Maharaja of Patiala leaned forward. His palm outstretched, he took a little of the powder as it fell like snow, and licked it.

Following his example, the Americans stood up and did the same, each one giving sincere thanks for the sacred ash.

'His Celestial Highness will now retreat,' Bitu said. 'He must pray for the Unloved Children.'

'Who are the Unloved Children?'

'The orphans His Holiness raises money to support

anonymously.'

Moved at the thought of such devotion, Rosco whispered something to Bitu, who whispered something back.

Then, fawning and thanking, the Americans departed.

Seated cross-legged on the hexagonal blanket, Omo-ji sat in silence, his eyes firmly closed.

In front of him, like fallen leaves, were thirty crisp hundred-dollar bills.

6

As SOON AS the American devotees were out of sight, the self-styled Maharaja of Patiala grabbed the money and danced about like Rumpelstiltskin.

'Told you it'd work!' he roared.

'*Shhhhhh*! They'll hear you!'

'They're long gone!'

Falling sideways, Harry rubbed his cramped legs.

'Quick – count it!'

Licking his thumb, Bitu shuffled through the notes fast.

'Three thousand dollars!'

'Jesus Christ!'

Clambering to their feet, they hugged each other and danced round and round.

'Time to go get a good meal,' said Bitu.

'Time to give half of it to charity,' Harry shot back.

'Better to do it back in Delhi.'

'What difference does it make?'

'Here at the Kumbh so-called charities are all scoundrels and fraudsters.'

Harry balked at the remark.

'Listen to what you're saying!'

'We're not tricksters,' Bitu retorted. 'We're just two lowly victims of theft.'

'Lowly people like a godman and his friend the Maharaja?!' Harry growled. 'Shame on you!'

Stiffening his shoulders, Bitu cleared his throat.

'What was I to do?' he asked, in the Maharaja's voice. 'They needed the sizzle of royalty to whet their appetites.'

7

LATE IN THE afternoon Harry and Bitu joined the streams of people trudging from the confluence to Allahabad Junction, a great many with bundles on their heads.

The communal sense of anticipation had gone, replaced by an air of tranquillity, as if sins and problems had been erased.

Neither Bitu nor Harry said a word on the way back to the station. Both were thinking of Omo-ji's performance and of the easy money they'd made. For Bitu it had been a thing of wonder – proof that vast spoils were ready and waiting for anyone bold enough to seize them.

Harry didn't share the same perspective.

He'd promised to give half the money to charity as soon as they reached the capital, and that's just what he intended to do. Having kept his promise, he planned to go to the British Embassy to apply for a replacement passport, and fly back to a new life in Blackpool, his soul cleansed of its curse.

The station was so packed they couldn't even get inside. Desperate to reach the platforms, literally millions of people were surging forwards, luggage on heads, and children held tight to chests.

'This is mad!' Harry yelled. 'There's no hope!'

'So what to do?'

'What about a bus?'

'They'll be just as bad! Kumbh Mela's ending and everyone wants to get home!'

The words having left his mouth, Bitu halted in his tracks, the waves of people pushing past.

'What the hell are you doing?' Harry yelled.

'Turn around – we'll go the other way.'

'Where?'

'Back to the river!'

Bitu had counted on the fact almost everyone attending the mass gathering had come from far away. Having set their hearts on getting to the ritual of a lifetime, pilgrims had bankrupted themselves to secure passage to the confluence at the appointed time. Most of them now faced the same prolonged journeys in reverse – almost all of them relied on overcrowded buses and trains.

Down at the pit-latrine, Bitu had heard a devotee describing how he'd come from the holy city of Varanasi – not by bus or train, but by boat.

By nightfall, they had reached the stretch of the Ganges from where dilapidated vessels plied the route downstream to India's most sacred city. Pleading with the ticket collector, Bitu swore there was an emergency. His dying father had been taken to the sacred city and that he had to get there to see him one last time. Taking pity on the pilgrims, the official waved them aboard without tickets.

Packed to at least twice its capacity, the boat was one of those disasters-in-waiting you hear about on the nightly news when it's capsized with all souls lost. In total darkness it chugged listlessly downstream, almost all the passengers forced to stand. The only ones afforded space were a cluster of dying pilgrims at the bow. Beside them lay an orderly row of bodies shrouded in white, their destination the Burning Ghats.

As the first light of dawn brought life to the twisting lanes of Varanasi, the vessel docked at the sacred city.

Unable to remember a more uncomfortable night, Harry staggered onto the jetty.

'I'm about to collapse,' he said.

'Let's get breakfast,' Bitu suggested.

'But we don't have any rupees.'

'We'll change the dollars.'

When the banks had opened, Bitu waited in line at the bureau de change, while his friend slumped on a broken plastic chair in the corner.

'It's no good, Harry-bhai,' he said forlornly. 'They're asking for a passport.'

'Tell them we were robbed!'

'I did. They don't care.'

'Damn them!'

'We'll use the black market,' Bitu said.

'Is it reliable?'

'Beggars can't be choosers, can they?!'

Leading the way to a backstreet, Bitu asked at one stall after another, but was met with a shaking head at each one.

'They don't want hundred-dollar bills,' he explained.

Harry pointed to an elaborate-looking *paan* stall at the end of the street.

'Let's ask there.'

Bitu stepped forward, the wad of notes in his hand. He asked the *paan* seller if he knew where to change foreign currency. A hand reached out and pointed at a well-dressed figure on the next street corner.

Hurrying over, Bitu showed the money and asked the rate.

The next thing he knew, both he and Harry had been handcuffed, and were being led to the police station.

An hour after that, they were sitting on the floor of a wretched cell with a huddle of pickpockets, fraudsters and other low-level criminals.

Having waited eight hours to be interviewed, they each gave a statement, which was typed in duplicate on an ancient manual typewriter. The money was confiscated in the name of evidence collection. Bitu and Harry were photographed, fingerprinted, and released with a stern caution to never again contravene the laws of Varanasi.

'Hate this country!' Bitu spat, the sentence sounding overly familiar.

'Bastards!' Harry moaned. 'Hope they all rot in Hell!'

'No breakfast or dinner now.'

'And no money for charity.'

'So what do we do?' Bitu asked. 'Wait for our luck to change.'

'Think it'll happen?'

'You never know,' Bitu said.

8

IN SILENCE THEY made their way down the steep stone steps to the ghats, the stark aprons of land on which the last cremations of the day were underway.

The narrow lanes of the old city were lined with beggars, many of them women dressed in white. Widowed in youth, a great many had been thrown out by their in-laws, before venturing to Varanasi, where they waited for death.

The ghats themselves were busy with pilgrims. Processing out of the river as the sun's light ebbed away, they sauntered off to pray at one of the multitude of temples. The evening air was filled with the peel of bells, with strains of invocation, and with the stench of burning wood, incense, and of the dead.

Unsure quite why they had been drawn forward, Harry and Bitu made their way along to the funeral pyres. Lined up beside each one, a dozen or more bereaved relatives were waiting their turn to complete the concluding ritual of life. An assortment of logs, roots, and misshapen branches were weighed out as handfuls of tattered rupee banknotes changed hands.

'Bloody depressing, isn't it?!' Bitu cackled.

Harry was about to say something, when a loud voice caused his friend to turn.

'Your Highness! Is that you, Your Highness?!'

Jerking into character, Bitu nudged Harry as he stepped forward to greet the only people in the world who regarded him as royalty.

The party of well-heeled Americans clustered around.

Doing a double-take, Bitu slipped into character and stretched out a hand out.

Instantly, it was kissed and blessed.

As soon as their aristocratic acquaintance had been showered in attention, Rosco enquired of Sri Omo-ji.

'His Celestial Highness has come to pray for the souls of the departed,' Bitu announced in an exuberant voice.

As if on cue, Harry fell to his knees and prayed at a stranger's funeral pyre blazing nearby. He was instantly bathed in the furnace-like heat, and in the pall of oily smoke from all the burning ghee.

Until that moment at the Burning Ghat, Harry had restrained himself, as though a dam wall were holding back a lifetime's worth of sin. But all at once, injustice and pain got the upper hand.

He remembered being bullied at school for wearing a turban, taunted by the other kids as a '*Paki!*'; being beaten by his mum for not getting A-grades, and by his dad for not respecting Guru Nanak. He relived the rejection: for not being of the East or the West; for not having the guts to come out to his family or friends; and for failing as a stage magician. All that before the recent torment of being robbed at the Kumbh Mela, being crushed to a pulp by pilgrims on both river and land, and being fleeced by Varanasi's police.

Kneeling there, his face to the fire and his back to the Americans, Harry recoiled in profound and absolute rage. From that moment on he resolved to do whatever it took to get his own back on the world – on everyone and everything.

9

AN HOUR LATER, the Maharaja of Patiala and His Celestial Highness Sri Omo-ji were reclining in a suite at the Taj Ganges Hotel, invited to stay as guests of the wealthy Americans from Tennessee.

Harry ordered three platters of room service. Having feasted, he soaked in a mammoth-sized tub, bubbles spilling over onto the marble floor. In the sitting-room,

Bitu lay sprawled out on the sofa, in his underpants, surfing channels on the giant-screen TV.

'Well, I'd say our luck's well and truly changed!' Harry yelled from the bathroom.

Chortling, Bitu clicked to the next channel. When his friend emerged, furled up in a luxurious bathrobe, he waved him over.

'Look at that bloody fraudster on TV!'

'Who?'

'Him!'

'*Who*?'

'That one! That man on the television!'

Peering at the screen, Harry struggled to make sense of what was going on.

A holy man was sitting on a dais in a cavernous meeting hall, his neck swathed in floral garlands, his wrist weighed down by a bejewelled Rolex.

'Who's he?' Harry asked.

'Told you, a bloody fraudster!'

'A *godman*?'

'Yes… he was doing "magic" a minute ago.'

'What kind?'

'Stopped his pulse, guessed a number in a sealed envelope… got out of a locked box.'

'Those are *my* tricks,' Harry said.

'But he's not doing them as tricks! He's performing them as miracles!'

Bitu pressed mute, and the two friends looked at one

another, both taking it as a sign of the path they must follow.

'It'll work!' Bitu snapped. 'We both know full well it will!'

Harry sighed, as though the world had slipped into sharp focus for the very first time.

'We'd have to plan it with great care, from the ground up,' he said.

The rest of the evening was spent brainstorming, and dreaming of potential reward.

On a pad of hotel notepaper Harry jotted down a to-do list:

1. Get start-up cash.

2. Create Sri Omo-ji's character from every possible angle. Hone it. Perfect it.

3. Seed rumours about him. Create large-scale hype.

4. Get a core following.

5. Work on social media and publicity.

6. Build on initial followers to gain wider appeal.

7. Study existing *sadhus*, gurus and godmen.

8. Keep the secret from everyone except Bitu-bhai.

With the list in his hand, Harry strode through into the bathroom in his boxers, his expression conveying determination. Fuelled by the same yearning for revenge he'd felt at the funeral pyre, he angled the shaving mirror towards the light. Peering at the magnified reflection of himself, he breathed in deep.

'I can do this!' he exclaimed. 'I can be Sri Omo-ji!'

10

EARLY NEXT MORNING a knock at the door jerked Harry from deep sleep.

With no sign of Bitu, he paced through into the sitting-room, and then to the hallway. A bellboy was standing to attention in the corridor, a crisp envelope in hand.

'A message, sir,' he said.

Taking it, Harry stepped back, closed the door, and admonished himself. A deity in human form would not do anything so menial as open the door to a member of hotel staff.

He ripped open the envelope and found a neatly handwritten letter inside. As he expected, it was from the Americans. Phrased in awkwardly florid language, the message enthused at what a great honour it was to cross paths with the dignitaries again. At the end of the message was a request.

His eyes wide, Harry rushed through into Bitu's room, pulled the curtains open and shook the bedding.

'Quickly, wake up! You've gotta see this, Bitu-bhai!'

Lost in dreamscape, Harry's friend groaned and cursed, before the blankets moved.

'What the heck!'

'Wake up!'

'Just five more minutes, this is a bloody first-rate dream!' Bitu muttered.

'No! Wake up! *Now!*'

In slow-motion Bitu sat up against the pillows, his face bloated and warm.

'What?' was all he could manage.

'The Americans have sent a message up.'

Bitu didn't reply. His breathing shallow, he blinked enquiringly.

'I'll cut to the best bit,' said Harry. '"Your Royal Highness, my friends and I do not wish to appear presumptive or out of line, but we would like to take advantage of what we regarded as a fortuitous meeting. Each one of us was touched in an overpowering way at being in the presence of His Celestial Highness. We felt His aura, His love, His pain, His beauty, and His prodigious sense of purpose. Please disregard this request if it goes against what you or He deems to be proper and correct. But if His Celestial Highness would consider it, my friends and I would be blessed beyond all reason were Sri Omo-ji to take us on as His pupils."'

Allowing the letter to fall onto the bed, Harry stared at his friend.

'It's the lock,' Bitu said.

'What lock?'

'The lock waiting for Sri Omo-ji's key.'

11

HARRY STEPPED OVER to the window and stared out at the army of sweepers preparing the Burning Ghats for another day.

'If we do this,' he said almost ferociously, 'we have to get things straight from the start.'

'His Celestial Highness can't be connected with Harry Singh, the son of a bone-chopper, the magician who flopped at the Blackpool Grand,' Bitu replied.

'I can't hide who I am – or who I've been!'

'You're gonna have to.'

'It's impossible – it'll get out.'

'Not if we keep everything watertight.'

Harry flinched.

'How the hell are we gonna do that?'

'By trusting no one, and by making sure we control every single detail.'

Harry slipped into an armchair beside the window.

'From now on I stay in character, at least when I'm with people who know me as Sri Omo-ji,' he said. 'I can't be calling down for room service and answering the door. In case you haven't noticed, living gods don't do that kind of stuff!'

Beneath the covers Bitu dug a hand down the front of his underpants and scratched himself long and hard.

'What about funding?'

'We spin a story to the Americans.'

'Think they'll cough up?'

'You saw how they're falling over themselves to be part of it!'

'It'll take some smooth talking from the Maharaja.'

Harry peered down at the floor.

'We're a start-up,' he said. 'We need investors to grow the business... and the best way to get investors is by giving them a sense that we know what we're doing.'

'They obviously liked the taster,' Bitu said.

'Yes they did, but we have to put them on hold – at least for the moment.'

'Whatever for? We've landed them – hook, line and sinker!'

'We're not ready!' Harry insisted. 'If we really are thinking big, then we have to plan it – step by step.'

'So what do we do with them in the meantime?'

'We send them on a sacred mission,' Harry said.

12

Taking a sheet of hotel letter paper from the rack, the Maharaja of Patiala wrote a message in his best handwriting, inviting Rosco to a private meeting in the hotel gardens at four that afternoon.

With time to spare, he slipped down to the line of high-end boutiques off the lobby, and picked up a new set of clothes for himself, putting it on the bill.

On the few occasions Bitu had ever met anyone halfway important, they were always late. So, although punctual by nature, he held off from venturing to the rendezvous until half past four.

'My apologies,' he said absently, crossing the last few feet of grass to where the American was sitting. 'His

Celestial Highness required my services.'

'Don't mention it,' Rosco intoned, kissing the back of the Maharaja's hand, adding: 'I do hope you are comfortable.'

Bitu smiled wryly.

'His Highness spent the entire night in meditation,' he said. 'But I admit I gave in to fatigue and squeezed in a couple of hours. I'm sure I'll go to Hell for it!'

His expression grave and sincere, Rosco from Tennessee swallowed hard.

'We wondered whether His Celestial Highness had a moment to consider our request,' he said.

The Maharaja smiled.

'He was deeply touched.'

'Oh, that's wonderful.'

'But...'

'*But*...?'

'But before His Highness can consider you for pupillage, He feels He must pray.'

Rosco nodded.

'Excellent, yes... I quite understand. If it's not too forward of me to enquire, how long will the prayer session go on?'

The Maharaja of Patiala gazed out into the distance.

'Fifteen days and fifteen hours,' he replied.

'Would it be helpful if we were to spend the time in prayer as well?'

Bitu shook his head.

'His Celestial Highness has made a suggestion,' he said.

'Of course, anything.'

'He would like you to prepare yourselves. Only once you have been prepared in the right way will His lessons be properly absorbed.'

Elated at being considered for the path of spiritual enlightenment, Rosco nodded earnestly.

'Absolutely,' he said. 'That makes complete sense.'

'The preparation will take the form of a journey,' the Maharaja explained. 'A Journey of Sacred Devotion.'

The American's eyes glazed over in wonder.

'Thank you!' he gasped.

'I will make sure the details are sent to you tonight,' the Maharaja of Patiala said, 'until then enjoy the last few hours of life untouched by the magic of Sri Omo-ji!'

13

FIVE MINUTES BEFORE midnight, an envelope was conveyed by the bellboy to Rosco's room, each corner marked with the number '6' in a circle.

Sitting on his bed, with his wife flapping over him, he read the message aloud:

'"As dictated by the Sixteenth Incarnation of His Celestial Highness Sri Omo-ji."'

'What does it say?' Rosco's wife asked fast.

'"Cherished Friends, we are bonded together by the sinews of love and peace, united as one being – hallowed and supreme in the eyes of Ultimate Truth. The confluence of the two great rivers, and the crossroads of humanity and faith, have brought us together at this auspicious moment. The preparation of your inner and outward forms will encompass six stages. Six is the number of salvation.'"

'Like the six sides of the blanket he was sitting on when we first met him,' Rosco's wife said.

'Listen... there's more: "You are to embark on a Journey of Sacred Devotion – visiting the six sacred places noted below. At each one, pray for the Unloved Children, watch for the signs, and feel my love in Untainted Truth.'"

Her eyes streaming in tears, Rosco's wife gave thanks for the blessing of Sri Omo-ji.

'I love him,' she said.

14

AT DAWN THE Americans departed on their Journey of Sacred Devotion.

As per orders, they wrote the number six in magic marker on the bottom of their feet, packed no perfume or after-shave, and told no one of their mission. Once all were seated in a rented tour bus, supplied by the hotel, Rosco stood at the front and addressed his friends.

'This is a special moment,' he said, his eyes welling with tears. 'His Celestial Highness has asked me to give details of our journey step by step. In no way am I better or more important than anyone else. I am merely the messenger. As His Celestial Highness has pointed out, we are all One.'

The Americans clapped.

'So where are we going?' one of them called out.

Rosco squinted at the letter sent by Sri Omo-ji.

'First stop is the Tree of Wisdom.'

'Where's that?'

'In Bihar.'

'What do we do there?'

'We pray for the Unloved Children, and look out for signs sent by Sri Omo-ji!' cried Rosco.

The driver eased the bus into gear, and steered out from the Taj Ganges.

Upstairs in their suite, Bitu and Harry stood at the window, like children watching their parents drive out of town. As soon as the vehicle turned onto the road, they did a high five.

A delicate knock at the door caused them to turn sharply round.

'You get it,' Harry said.

'Think they're onto us?' Bitu whispered.

'Go find out.'

Slipping into character, the Maharaja of Patiala pulled the door open, smiling demurely at the attendant.

'Excuse me Your Highness, but an American asked for this envelope to be brought up.'

Giving thanks, Bitu took the packet, his fingers squeezing it. A moment later, he was opening it, Harry watching in tense silence.

'It's a letter to me.'

'What does it say?'

'"As I feel unable to address His Celestial Highness directly on account of his elevated status as a living god, I would be indebted if you could make sure the enclosed donation is used to help the Unloved Children. Yours sincerely, Rosco P Schultz III."'

'Rosco P Schultz *the third*?'

'That's what it says,' Bitu answered, sliding the contents of the packet onto his hand – two stacks of hundred-dollar notes bound with mustard-coloured bands.

'*Christ!*'

Bitu inhaled as if starved of oxygen.

'Look! That's $10,000 printed on each band!'

Harry slumped on the sofa.

'We've gotta stay focused,' he said. 'It's the only way to keep to the plan.'

'You sure we can trust the driver?'

'Course we can. Luckily he's a Sikh… We Sikhs look out for Sikhs,' Harry said assuredly. 'And, anyway, you gave him all that loot from the gift shop.'

'When's he going to call?'

'Each evening at dusk.'

Jabbing the money up to his nose, Bitu inhaled the

aroma as though he were smelling a bouquet of fresh roses.

'God, I love greenbacks!' he snorted.

15

Lumbering back to the suite with half a dozen shopping bags in his hands, Bitu blushed.

'Got the money changed,' he said, 'and went shopping. Charged a few outfits... to *Rosco's* account. Feel guilty at taking liberties.'

'I wouldn't bother,' Harry said.

'Wouldn't bother going shopping?'

'Wouldn't bother feeling bad.'

'Why not?'

Harry held up his iPhone.

'Rosco P Schultz III.'

'What about him?'

'He's a tech billionaire!'

Bitu pressed a hand to his mouth and swallowed anxiously.

'Is that good?'

'I'd say it is!' Harry shot back. 'Made his fortune in microchips. Started an empire from his garage and sold it last month for three billion bucks.'

'That must be why he's in India.'

'It is. He's come to find himself. But more importantly, he's come to find a guru.'

'How d'you know that?' Bitu asked.

'Read it in *The Economist*,' Harry said.

16

FOLLOWING INSTRUCTIONS, BHALU, the driver, made a detour into the modest town of Dehri on the banks of the Sone River.

While his American passengers stretched their legs, ate *dosas* for lunch, took photographs of the temples, and said prayers for the Unloved Children, he did exactly as he'd been ordered to do.

Before trooping back onto the bus, Rosco dodged bicycles and rickshaws to cross the street for a pack of gum. His thoughts were on Sri Omo-ji and on the holy man's aura of unflinching selflessness. Fishing a five-hundred-rupee note from his pocket, he handed it over to the owner of a *paan* stall. As he took the change, his attention focused on something pasted to the stall's sign.

An orange card bearing the number 6 in a stylized hexagon.

'My goodness! What's that?' he cried, jabbing a hand at the symbol.

The *paan* seller held a finger to his lips.

'Sri Omo-ji is love,' he said.

When Rosco told the others of his discovery, they hurried across the road amid the onslaught of traffic to see the symbol for themselves.

'It's a sign that He's with us in spirit,' declared Marsha.

'Of course He is,' her husband said. 'Even though I

can't see Him, I can feel Him.'

'Yes, yes!' Marsha agreed. 'I feel His energy, too.'

'He's always with me,' Rosco murmured, taking a selfie with the symbol, a hand touched to his chest. 'He's right here in my heart.'

17

UP IN THE suite, Harry and Bitu had turned the sitting-room into a prospective godman's nerve centre, the floor covered with sheets of paper.

They had spent most of the day working on a flowchart, mapped out messily in marker pen. His hand tired from scribbling notes, Harry grabbed a fresh sheet and listed key words for the hundredth time:

1. Magic
2. Belief
3. Publicity
4. Funding

Pacing up and down on the other side of the room, Bitu cleared his sinuses, retched, and held up a hand.

'We need an ashram,' he said.

'You mean a headquarters?'

'Yes. You see, without one a godman is free-floating. And free-floating godmen have no chance at all.'

'We can't get an ashram just like that,' Harry responded.

'Why not? We've got Rosco the Third.'

'We have to reel him in slowly. Only then will we be

able to sink our teeth into him.'

'You mean, into his money?'

Harry looked over at his friend and shrugged.

'Same thing.'

'So what's the best way to reel Rosco in?'

'By giving him something.'

'But he can bloody well afford anything he wants.'

'Not like that. You saw how moved he was by the Dreamseed.'

'You mean that silly plastic bead?'

'Meant the world to him.'

'Stupid bloody idiot,' said Bitu.

'You're right, he can get anything he wants,' Harry answered. 'But I'm not talking about material stuff. I'm talking about the kind of thing you can't put a price on.'

'Like?'

'Like Love, Joy, Wisdom.'

'He's sure to see through it,' Bitu said softly.

Harry shrugged again.

'Don't be so sure. We've messed around for a couple of days and look at what we've landed. If we hone our game and do it right, just imagine what rich pickings we'll be in line for!'

Bitu went over to the coffee table and marvelled at the neat stacks of thousand-rupee notes covering its surface.

'I say that we grab the cash and split right now!'

'*No!*' Harry yelled. 'Out of the question! I've waited my entire life for this.'

'For a billionaire stupid enough to give you envelopes stuffed with greenbacks?'

'For someone to respect me,' Harry replied.

18

THE TOUR BUS reached the Mahabodhi Mahavihara Temple at Bodh Gaya late in the afternoon.

Since spotting the secret hexagonal sign, the American passengers were unable to think of anything but the guru's aura. As they saw it, if Sri Omo-ji's presence was felt at such a random and insignificant *paan* stall, the holy man was surely far more celebrated than modesty allowed him to admit.

Clambering out of the bus, Bhalu the driver took them to see the sacred tree beneath which Buddha is said to have received Enlightenment. The spot was the first stage on their Journey of Sacred Devotion. While the foreigners were lining up to buy tickets, the driver made his way to the sacred tree, as he had been instructed to do.

A few minutes later, Rosco and the rest of the group reached the sacred spot, said to be the Navel of the Earth.

'It's so special,' enthused Marsha.

'I can feel Him here,' Rosco broke in. 'Don't know how or why, but I feel Sri Omo-ji's aura in the shadow of the tree, as though He's embracing us.'

'*Look*!' Fred yelled, pointing through the fence.

Clustering around, the group fixed their gaze on the

detail Fred was pointing to.

Another orange card featuring a hexagon, the number 6 drawn inside.

One of the women, Helen, broke into tears.

'We are *so* blessed!' she sobbed.

'So blessed to have a path of true love,' Fred added.

'He needs us,' Rosco whispered, the words heavy with a sense of duty. 'We must help Him.'

'And we must help the Unloved Children,' Marsha added firmly.

That evening the driver called in with his first update.

'They saw two of the cards but missed the others,' he reported.

'How many did you place?' Bitu demanded.

'Almost twenty, sir.'

'One in ten – not a bad start. Make them more obvious next time, OK?'

'Yes, yes, sir.'

'Tomorrow take them to the Great Stupa in Nalanda. Do you understand?'

'Yes, sir!'

'Be sure to distribute a lot more cards! Put them in places where they're definitely going to see them, OK?'

Nodding into the phone, Bhalu hung up the call.

'Two out of twenty,' said Bitu.

'I reckon they need to find three or four a day to stay interested,' Harry answered. 'The danger's if one of them spots Bhalu dropping the cards.'

'That would ruin us.'

Standing up, Harry stepped over to the mosaic-rimmed mirror hanging above the desk, and took a good long look at himself.

'We're only scratching the surface,' he said.

'*Meaning*?'

'Meaning that in order to carry this off, I have to be him.'

'But you are him.'

'No, I'm not. I have to be him inside and out.'

Bitu grinned.

'You want to change your name by deed poll?'

'No,' Harry replied in a cold tone. 'Not like that. Not become him on paper, but become him in my blood and my bones.'

'And how to do that?'

'By living him.'

'You're talking nonsense Harry-bhai.'

'No, I'm not. For once I'm talking the most perfect truth.'

19

NEXT DAY, A pair of trademark orange cards were discovered by the Americans while touring the Great Stupa at Nalanda.

The night before, Rosco had been visited by the guru in a curious dream. Sri Omo-ji had been standing in a field of corn somewhere in Nebraska. The right half of his body had been painted red and the left side, green. On his head he'd been balancing a flowerpot in which sixteen electric eels were swimming. Keeping the dream to himself, he didn't want the others to feel as though he'd been singled out for special attention.

While the Americans were holding a special roadside prayer session for the Unloved Children, Harry immersed himself in key information.

He trawled the Internet for everything he could find about godmen, *yogis*, *sadhus*, gurus, and all the rest. Listing their eccentricities, whims, and phobias, he noted down their favourite foods, obsessions, and the catalogue of tricks they passed off as miracles. The most useful information of all was gleaned from the Netflix sensation *Wild Wild Country*, detailing the rise and fall of Bhagwan Rajneesh, AKA Osho.

Poring through hundreds of sites, something struck Harry: India's home-grown breed of living gods professed to be uninterested in their own welfare. It was the one thing they all made known. But the truth was quite the opposite – that they were completely and utterly self-centred.

By pushing away devotees, gifts, and all the attention, they were in actual fact welcoming it all. In return they provided something no amount of money could ever buy – a talisman against human insecurity.

Once another room service banquet had been devoured, Harry took a long hot bath, in which he pondered the state of affairs.

Wrapped in a luxurious bathrobe, he wandered through to the sitting-room, where Bitu was sitting over a brand-new laptop.

'I've worked out the secret,' Harry said.

'Which secret?'

'The alchemical secret that turns mere mortals into real godmen.'

'What are you talking about, Harry-bhai?'

'The secret that'll transform me from Harry Singh into His Celestial Highness Omo-ji.'

Bitu groaned.

'What is it?'

'Aloofness,' Harry replied.

'*Aloof*...?'

'*Ness*. I've got to appear detached.'

'That's it? That's the secret?'

'Yup. I've studied every godman from here to San Francisco and they're all aloof.'

'So what does the aloofness mean?'

'It means godmen are detached... they're not ruled by the laws of society.'

'Because they're not human?'

'Exactly.'

Bitu typed in 'Top Indian godmen', and did an

image search. The laptop's screen came alive with a full range of pictures – clean-shaven gurus and others with luxuriant beards; old gurus and young; gurus wearing turbans, floral crowns, and even beanies; gurus in red robes, orange robes, in pink and in blue; lone naked gurus, and others garlanded in flowers and surrounded by hordes of sycophantic devotees.

'The question's how to get anyone to take notice of Sri Omo-ji,' Bitu said. 'Look for yourself – the godman business is already crowded.'

Harry waved the Google search away.

'We'll get followers by not trying to get them,' he said.

'No one will give us the time of day.'

'Yes they will.'

'How?'

'Sri Omo-ji will be different,' Harry replied.

'How?'

'Because he'll appeal to everyone.'

'To everyone in India?'

'Everyone *everywhere*! North, south, west and east! He'll bridge values and cultures, raise money for good causes…'

'And make people laugh,' said Bitu resolutely. 'Because laughter's important.'

'Sure – Sri Omo-ji will make people cry with laughter! And he'll sing to them in a way they've never been sung to before!'

'There's something I'm still not understanding.'

'What?'

Bitu tapped a black and white picture. It showed a godman in abundant robes on the stage of an American stadium.

'How do we go from a hotel room in Varanasi to Madison Square Garden?'

'We do it by planning bigger than big!' Harry replied.

20

NEXT STOP ON the Journey of Sacred Devotion was Kolkata's South Park Street Cemetery.

Dating back to the East India Company, the burial ground was once on the outskirts of the original capital of the British Raj. At a time when administrators tended to drop dead from tuberculosis, malaria, and dysentery, often soon after their arrival, the cemetery filled up within little more than twenty years.

Clambering out of the bus, the American group toured the burial ground in awe, details of short colonial lives etched in the imposing stone monoliths.

'I wonder why His Celestial Highness wanted us to come here,' Fred remarked gloomily. 'It's as grim as anything I've ever seen.'

'I think it's magnificent!' Helen announced.

'It's a sign,' said Rosco P Schultz III. 'A sign for us to remember that nothing lives forever.'

Reading one of the marble plaques, Marsha frowned. 'These guys didn't live long.'

'That's it!' Rosco countered. 'That's the message: Life isn't about the age you get to before you go – but about the goodness inside you.'

'Wow! What a powerful message!' Felicity said, eyes wide in wonder.

'To think that Sri Omo-ji transmitted it through a few old stones,' Rosco's brother-in-law, Marvin, whispered.

Standing to the right of him, Marsha was about to reply, when her friend Mary-Lou hurried over.

'Found one! Found one!' she wailed, holding up one of the orange cards.

'He walks with us,' Fred said.

'He *is* us,' Elaine added.

His expression pained, Rosco turned to the others.

'I miss Him more strongly than anything I've ever known,' he said.

21

AT THE PRECISE moment the Americans were pining for their guru in South Park Street Cemetery, he was emerging from the bathroom.

'Take any more baths and your skin will start coming off!' Bitu spat.

'I'm going to write a book,' Harry replied.

'*Book*? What book?'

'A holy book. One to rival those of the great faiths. It'll explain to Sri Omo-ji's followers what he stands for.'

Bitu looked up in horror.

'It'll take bloody weeks to write a book!' he yelled. 'And in any case you can't bloody type!'

'I'll dictate it into my phone and get it transcribed.'

'Well you better get a move on!'

Harry sighed.

'Jesus Christ! It's all *go go go* for a godman!'

Pacing through into his bedroom, Harry stretched out on the king-sized bed, iPhone in hand. Lids lowering over his eyes, he collected his thoughts, cleared his throat, and the dictation began:

'The Testament by His Celestial Highness Sri Omo. Chapter One: Divine Fate. A wise fool was once asked by a traveller how it was that he cowered in terror when walking beneath an oak tree. "Because to ants, acorns are like cannon balls falling from the sky!" he replied. "But you are not an ant," the traveller responded. "Thank god for that," the fool quipped, "for if I were, I wouldn't be standing here talking to you now!"'

As Harry dictated *The Testament*, Bitu worked on designing a structure for 'The Path of Omo', drawing from the brainstorming sessions and the mass of scribbled notes.

He may have spent more than thirty years in England, but the subcontinent was inside him in a way that second-generation Indians could never quite grasp. For Bitu, India wasn't about the poverty and the noise, or the full assault on the senses. Rather, it was about being self-assured in a rock solid and inexplicable way.

Sourcing experts online, Bitu put together a team of branding and social media specialists, graphic designers, stylists, marketing people, and a legion of logistical staff.

Every hour or so, he'd take a break from work, go over to the cupboard, and open the wall safe. The single most powerful motivating force he knew was the smell of money – a glorious reminder there was everything to play for.

While his friend drooled over the bricks of cash and put together the team, Harry's dictation got into its stride.

After lunch, he cleared his throat, took a sip of iced Perrier, and continued:

'Chapter Six: Mastery. The only word I can speak with complete and utter devotion is LOVE. Not the false love of the mass media age, but the love that's in the eyes of a mother who holds her newborn baby for the first time. The love which seduces us. The love that holds us to account and bewitches each and every one of us. A love which never tires. The love that gives and does not take…'

All of a sudden, Bitu barged in.

'Stop! Stop!'

'But I'm dictating! I'll lose my thread.'

'You gotta stop!'

'Why?'

'Because there's a problem… a BIG problem!'

'What?'

'Bhalu just called.'

'Great. What's the update?'

Bitu's face seized up in horror.

'The tour bus has crashed!'

'*Jesus*! Are any of them injured?'

'Not sure.'

'What happened?'

'A water truck hit them.'

'Where?'

'Calcutta.'

Harry bit his knuckle.

'Time for damage limitation,' he said.

An hour later, Bhalu phoned with a garbled update: the Americans were shaken and bruised, but there were no broken bones. They'd clambered aboard a new tour bus. Unable to carry on the Journey of Sacred Devotion, they were heading to the airport for the short flight back to Varanasi.

'We don't have much time!' Harry said fast. 'Need to think on our feet.'

'Got the whole team branding Sri Omo-ji,' Bitu replied. 'We need more time.'

Harry closed his eyes, his mind flooding with godspeak.

'We've got to get out of here,' he said.

'What?!'

'Leave.'

'When?'

'Now!'

'But I like it here!' Bitu answered in distress.

'Course you do. Me too. But it's too obvious.'

Bitu frowned.

'And what's less obvious, Harry-bhai?'

'Giving them a trail to follow.'

'We already have – the Journey of Sacred Devotion.'

'Not that. Another trail. A trail leading to Sri Omo-ji.'

'What if they're so knocked about they want to get back home to America?'

'Then it'll test us,' Harry said. 'If we can hold on to Rosco P Schultz III and his band of merry men then I'll have passed the test.'

'What test?'

'The test of being a pukka godman!'

PART III

1

WHEN THE AMERICANS had arrived battered and bruised from the airport, the concierge presented them with an envelope.

Clustering around, they listened as Rosco read the letter written hastily on hotel paper:

'His Celestial Highness wishes you to know He has been praying for your souls. Having witnessed suffering and pain, He travelled across the Desert of Torment, and is waiting for you at The Great Stone. Respectfully yours, Maharaja Patiala.'

'The Great Stone?' said Rosco, repeating the words again. 'Wonder where that is.'

'Let's think about it tomorrow,' Marsha moaned. 'I need a bath and a good night's sleep.'

'You guys go ahead to your rooms,' Rosco replied. 'I'm gonna go talk to the concierge and see what we can come up with.'

While the Americans settled back into the lap of luxury, the Maharaja and the godman hurried through Varanasi on a rickshaw to a rendezvous...

A rendezvous with a fixer found online named 'Zap'.

Although only five foot one, what he lacked in stature was made up in verve. Zap was waiting at the roadside tea stall, an impressive handlebar moustache concealing much of his face. Even though the sun wasn't bright, he was wearing extra-dark Ray-Ban Aviators. In his right hand was a clipboard, and in his left, a pair of iPhones.

Having introduced himself as the Maharaja of Patiala, and his associate as His Celestial Highness Sri Omo-ji, Bitu cleared his throat.

'We need to work fast,' he said.

Zap, the fixer, whose website bragged he could 'fix the unfixable', tilted his glasses down and peered over them.

'Trouble with the police?' he asked quizzically.

'No, no... nothing like that.'

'Then may I ask what is the reason for your hurry?'

'We've got some American friends visiting in a day or two and we want to get everything ready for them.'

'We need an ashram,' Harry said, recoiling as Bitu kicked him under the table.

'What His Holiness means is that we need a quiet place to hold a retreat.'

The fixer who could fix the unfixable, sniffed.

'I can help you,' he said, 'But...'

'But what?'

'But you have to tell me the truth,' he said.

'I *am* telling you the truth,' Bitu shot back.

Zap looked at the pair and shook his head, his expression unconvinced.

'I have been doing this work a long time,' he said. 'In that time I've met every kind of person you can think of – from beggars to world leaders. In all the years I have been a fixer, it's my sense of smell that's developed above everything else.'

'Don't understand what you mean,' Bitu replied.

'What I am saying is that I'm not smelling a maharaja and a guru – but rather two well-meaning charlatans.'

Bitu leapt to his feet.

'How dare you?' he roared, his aristocratic accent slipping.

Zap the fixer didn't flinch. Picking up one of his phones, he typed something in fast, squinted at a photo, and grinned.

'The Maharaja of Patiala doesn't quite look like you,' he said, holding the screen up.

'It's a mix-up,' Bitu stammered, his face warming in a blush.

'Shall I look up His Celebrationary Highness?'

'His *Celestial* Highness!' Harry corrected. 'Do anything you like. We're leaving!'

'Tell me the truth and I will help you,' said Zap.

2

OVER A SECOND cup of milky masala tea, Bitu and Harry came clean. They had no other choice.

In return, the fixer made a promise.

'I swear to you that I will never spill the beans,' he said.

'How can we be sure?' Harry asked.

'Because a fixer is only as good as his reputation,' Zap replied.

Bitu looked at him ferociously.

'If you betray us,' he said, 'I will hunt you for the rest of time.'

'Tell me what you need,' the fixer said.

'Miracles,' Harry answered.

'Miracles at double-speed,' Bitu chipped in.

Without wasting a moment, Zap typed a message to his network.

Three and a half minutes passed, and one of the phones chimed.

'Perfect,' he said, reading the text.

Still bristling at having gone against their plan so soon, Bitu shrugged.

'What is?'

'The ashram I've found you.'

Piling into Zap's battered white Ambassador car, they drove a short distance from the Varanasi Cantonment. The vehicle rolled up outside a disused boarding school.

A sorrowful man was waiting at the gates.

Introducing himself as Hirundi K Bapu, his head was crowned with the king of comb-overs and he was stuffed into a charcoal suit three sizes too small.

'The school was recently shut down by the authorities,' he explained awkwardly. 'Some trouble with a teacher who didn't keep his hands to himself. The parents were up in arms – said that if the place wasn't shut down they'd lynch the staff.'

Hirundi K Bapu gave a full tour of the premises – taking in the numerous classrooms and the science labs, the dormitories, kitchens, gymnasium, and a dining hall large enough to house a cargo plane.

Touching the side of his hand to the top of his head, he fanned the strands of hair outwards in a well-practised movement.

'This way to the main hall,' he said.

Having taken an underground corridor, they popped up behind the stage of an enormous auditorium.

Harry nudged Bitu in the ribs.

'This is frigging perfect!' he whispered. 'Ask him the price!'

By the end of the afternoon, a contract had been drawn up with a month's rent paid in cash. As soon as Mr Bapu had driven away, the Maharaja of Patiala thrust a list of bullet points at the fixer's chest.

'We need all this done ASAP!'

Rolling his dark glasses up onto his head, Zap perused the list. The tip of his finger running down the entries, he mumbled a string of numbers.

'Twenty-three *lakhs*,' he said.

'That's bloody highway robbery!' Bitu cursed.

Calming his friend, Harry looked at the fixer, his face mirrored in Ray-Ban lenses.

'If we pay you half now, and half later, when can you have it ready?'

The fixer scratched the back of his head.

'By five pm tomorrow afternoon,' he said.

3

HIDING FROM THE Americans in a bid to raise their stock value, Harry and Bitu took a room in a modest guest house on the banks of the Ganges, and worked through the night.

Phone in hand, and firmly in character, Sri Omo-ji sat on his bed dictating at lightning speed. By clearing his mind, he found he could spew an unending barrage of spiritual gobbledygook – the kind that was the communal currency of the gurus he'd seen preaching on YouTube.

A few feet away, his friend was busy hiring Two-See, a Chinese social media expert, to get the mother of all campaigns underway. As with everyone and everything else, Two-See was paid by transferring funds through Hawali, a peer-to-peer system dating back centuries. A bundle of cash handed to a street-stall broker in Varanasi could be paid out reliably by another low-level broker just about anywhere.

Operating from a rabbit-hutch flat on the bad side of Shenzhen, Two-See set up Sri Omo-ji accounts on the main social media platforms, and seeded hundreds of leads all over the Internet.

'Those bloody Chinese can make anything happen!' Bitu cackled. 'They're the future of the godman business!'

Harry broke off from dictating.

'Forgotten where I was,' he said in exasperation.

'Doesn't really matter... just say the word "love" a hundred times and then launch into it again.'

'That's ridiculous.'

'No it's not – it's "spirituality".'

With a sigh, Harry tapped *record*, and said:

'Love, love...'

4

THE KUMBH MELA may have been over, but it was days before the crowds were gone.

Marney, the friendly Canadian who'd sought enlightenment at the monumental gathering of humanity, had planned to travel down to Mumbai by way of the capital. But after three days of waiting at Allahabad Junction he gave up hope of ever getting aboard a train. Downhearted, he slung his backpack onto his shoulders and strolled out to the open road.

A constant stream of pilgrims was still trudging towards the station, bundles on their heads. Many more were walking along the open road towards some distant destination. Unsure of what to do, Marney followed them.

After three days of hiking and zigzagging rides, he clambered off a truck laden with newly picked cotton on the outskirts of Varanasi. All he could think were the words spoken by his mother as he left home:

'You'll know the path to follow, Marney my love. The only way to find it is to be true to yourself.'

5

As STRAIGHT-BACKED AS he was immaculate, the chief concierge at the Taj Ganges was a Goan Christian named David X David.

Having worked at the hotel for as long as anyone could remember, he prided himself on having memory second to none. He never forgot a guest's name or face – even if years elapsed between visits. When asked for specific information he would draw upon his vast network, and provide answers in faultless detail.

While the rest of his group soaked in bubble baths, Rosco P Schultz III quizzed the concierge on what he knew about the Great Stone.

Although expert in all matters relating to the holy city, David X David was baffled.

'If you would not mind, sir, please give me until tomorrow morning at eight,' he replied. 'On my mother's grave I promise to have the information you require by then.'

Five minutes before the deadline, David X David was pacing up and down, fearful he was about to fail the distinguished American guest. No one in his extensive network had any idea about the Great Stone.

Resigning himself to failure, the concierge reproached himself for failing. Across the lobby, the lift counted down from the ninth floor – undoubtedly Mr Schultz from Suite 925.

His mouth dry, David X David watched the lift's door open. Schultz stepped out and began strolling towards the concierge desk.

His feet were halfway across the polished marble floor of the lobby when David X David's phone buzzed. Glancing at the screen, the concierge quickly read a text:

THE GREAT STONE CAN BE FOUND
AT THE FOLLOWING ADDRESS:
457 GULL MARG, VARANASI.
THE AUSPICIOUS MOMENT TO
VIEW IT IS 6 PM.

6

ON THE DOT of five, Harry and Bitu arrived at the school by rickshaw, half-expecting it to be deserted and boarded up.

But to their astonishment, Zap the fixer who could fix the unfixable, was a man of his word.

The school's sign had been replaced by an outsized symbol – the number 6 within a hexagon. The sacred emblem was repeated everywhere – painted on the walls, etched into the windows, and even arranged in flowers out in the garden.

An army of nocturnal cleaners, moonlighting from a nearby power station, had cleaned the school building from top to bottom. The gardens had been landscaped by a platoon of gardeners borrowed from Varanasi's Radisson Hotel. Fountains which hadn't worked in years had been conjured back to life, and banners bearing the buzzwords of Sri Omo-ji were suspended from all the walls, inside and out.

In back rooms dozens of uniformed staff were busy planning projects and prayer sessions, and pretending to send messages to the godman's followers all over the world. In the kitchens dinner was being prepared by a legion of cooks. As for the great hall, it was awash with floral arrangements, giant-sized candles, and incense burners perched on elaborate stands.

Sitting on the floor cross-legged and reverent were more than three hundred orange-clad disciples. Hanging around the neck of each was a garland of pungent *mogra* flowers, and a circular framed photo of Sri Omo-ji, the diameter of a coffee mug.

'What are they doing?' Bitu asked, a hint of trepidation in his voice.

'Praying for the soul of our beloved Sri Omo-ji,' the fixer said cheerily.

'Who *are* they?'

'A handful of the city's homeless... happy to perform round-the-clock prayers in return for clean clothes and a little food. On safety grounds I promised each and every one of them a free health check, too.'

'Health check... *where*?' Bitu asked.

'In the medical centre, down the hall.'

Harry grabbed Zap's hand and shook it very hard.

'How did you do it in such a short time?' he asked,

perplexed.

Eyes hidden behind the extra-dark lenses, the fixer replied:

'Wait till you see the MZ.'

'What's that?'

'The Meditation Zone.'

Zap may have exceeded all expectations, but Bitu was fretful.

'There's no stone,' he said.

'Stone?' Harry echoed. 'What stone?'

'The Great Stone.'

'Doesn't matter, Bitu-bhai... he's got everything else.'

The fixer held up a hand.

'Two minutes,' he said.

'For what?'

Leading the way out to the front of the school, Zap pointed at an area of wet cement, then up into the sky. A rock the approximate size and shape of a forty-foot sea container was dangling from the end of a steel cable. Etched on each of the four sides in five-foot-high letters, was the sacred symbol of Sri Omo-ji.

As they watched, it was lowered to earth, along with an exquisite wrought iron bench.

The fixer smoothed a hand down over his handlebar moustache.

'There it is... the Great Stone.'

As if on cue, his phone buzzed with a message from David X David at the Taj Ganges.

'The Americans are on their way.'

Cool as a cucumber, he reached into his pocket, pulled out a miniature air-horn and gave it two long bursts.

'What's that for?' Harry asked.

'All systems go!'

Bitu whacked Harry on the back.

'Quick, go do your godspeak in the auditorium!'

'But what shall I say?'

'Just pretend you're reading from *The Path of Omo*!'

7

TAKING A HOLDALL with the second half of his fee, Zap the fixer hurried out through the back entrance, while Bitu scurried to the bench beside the Great Stone.

As the seat of his jodhpurs touched the wrought iron, he heard feet crunching over freshly raked gravel.

Still battered and bruised, the Americans reached the stone, Rosco P Schultz III in the lead.

'Your Highness!' he boomed. 'What experiences we've had, and what an honour it is to see you again!'

Stepping forward to the bench, he kissed the Maharaja's knuckles, as did the others, each waiting their turn.

The Maharaja of Patiala explained how witnessing the trauma of the crash in Kolkata, His Celestial Highness had experienced their pain.

'Our wounds are healing,' Rosco replied merrily.

'What *is* this place?' Marsha asked in awe.

'The sacred retreat of His Celestial Highness Sri Omo-ji,' the Maharaja answered with a stone-cold poker face.

'I wish we'd known of it before,' Marsha blurted out.

'The ashram is regarded as a hallowed ground,' the Maharaja answered, 'and only those who His Highness believes have earned it are admitted.'

The Americans appeared crestfallen.

'But we didn't finish the Journey of Sacred Devotion,' said Elaine. 'Does that mean we're not allowed to enter?'

Standing, the Maharaja prefaced his reply with an ear-to-ear grin.

'On the contrary my dear lady,' he announced, 'you have all proved yourselves worthy of the highest regard. His Highness welcomes you to His humble home, and asks that you relax and make yourselves comfortable.'

The group exchanged anxious glances.

'But we don't want to relax!' Rosco declared.

'We want to help the Unloved Children!' another yelled.

'There'll be time for that,' Bitu intoned. 'But first you must perform the sacred ritual of honouring the Great Stone.'

Elaine pushed her way to the front.

'Would you tell us the ritual, Your Highness?' she asked.

Even before the question had left her mouth, the Maharaja of Patiala was demonstrating the curious ceremonial circumambulation of the sacred rock. Walking around it backwards, he pressed both hands to its surface with every other step, and let out a sound resembling the woeful lament of an Arctic wolf howling in the night.

Without a word, the Americans fell into line, copying the ritual as precisely as they could manage. Having circled the Great Stone backwards six times, the Maharaja of Patiala gave thanks to the heavens for His Celestial Highness Sri Omo-ji.

Dutifully, the Americans did the same.

8

TWO THOUSAND MILES from the ashram, Two-See the Internet maestro in Shenzhen was putting the final touches to a world-class media campaign.

Having received the audio file, he had *The Path of Omo* digitally transcribed in Honolulu, proofread by an impoverished undergraduate at Cambridge, and typeset in Chennai. Within a matter of hours the godman's spiritual manifesto was for sale on Amazon.

Two-See used the text as the basis of a wide-reaching social media campaign – on Twitter, Instagram, Facebook, Reddit, and on dozens of other platforms. Unlike other media gurus, Two-see relied on a piece of software he'd designed himself which he referred to as XING-92. Cloaked in secrecy, the program enabled Two-See to ensure any message posted went instantly viral, by hacking into a person's social media accounts.

Within minutes of going live, *The Path of Omo* had been seen by millions. A leading inspirator in Los Angeles heralded it as 'An Extraordinary Solution to the Ordinary'. Another claimed 'it was like having a bucket of ice-water thrown over me'.

News of the book went viral.

Posts hyped it from Adelaide to Alaska, as it plugged a gap in the market of literary godspeak.

9

HAVING DUMPED HIS backpack at the Ganpati Guest House, Marney the Canadian roamed through the telescoping backstreets of ancient Varanasi, and found himself at Manikarnica, the Burning Ghat.

As on every afternoon, the recently deceased were being borne on funeral pyres, the closest male relative stepping up at the appointed moment to crack the skull in order for the soul to be released.

Moved by the scene, and with the lengthening shadows edging towards dusk, Marney strolled solemnly along the waterline, and back to his guest house. Up on the roof terrace he pondered life and death, then sent a message to his best friend back in Toronto, which read:

'India: Light in a World of Darkness.'

Marney posted a selfie from Varanasi on Instagram. Before clicking off his phone, a quote caught his eye:

'He is Light in a World of Darkness.'

Recoiling in wonder, he checked the source and discovered it was linked to His Celestial Highness Sri Omo-ji.

A minute after that, Marney had read his way through the holy man's Wikipedia page – which had gone live eight minutes before. To his delight, he learned the holy man had an ashram in Varanasi, at The Great Stone.

'It's a sign,' Marney said under his breath. 'I must go to him at once.'

10

WHEN THE BACKWARDS circumambulation had been completed, and the sacred blessing to Sri Omo-ji made, Rosco P Schultz III addressed the Maharaja on behalf of the group.

'We don't wish to impose, Your Highness,' he said, 'but would it be possible to get a tour of the ashram?'

His stomach churning in trepidation, Bitu dipped his head cordially.

'Of course, I would be more than honoured to show you around,' he said.

Turning, he led the way from the Great Stone, across what had recently been the playground. As they neared the main school building, the door opened and a woman dressed in saffron-orange robes emerged. Like everyone else, she had a photograph of the guru hanging around her neck. Young, pretty, and seductively charming, she greeted the Maharaja.

'Excuse me, Your Highness,' she said gently, 'but His Celestial Highness Sri Omo-ji has asked for you to meet Him in the Hall of Unconditional Love. If you would not mind, I would be pleased to give the distinguished visitors a tour of the campus.'

Both feet rooted to the ground, Bitu sensed time stop in freeze-frame. As if observing the situation from above, he marvelled how Zap the fixer had even fixed a guide to appear at the exact moment she was needed.

'Thank you...' the Maharaja said, straining to appear solemn.

'*Karnika*, Your Highness.'

'Thank you Karnika... I'll attend His Celestial Highness at once.'

11

DRESSING IN THE elaborate saffron robes and matching turban which the fixer had left for him in the green room behind the stage, Harry was suffering from a terrible bout of nerves.

He caught a flash of himself about to step out to a packed house at the Blackpool Grand on the night of his monumental fall from grace. On that inauspicious evening the casket had not opened. But, as Harry reflected, the fact that it hadn't had allowed this new reality to take shape, with fresh doors opening in all directions.

The memory of failure was melted by another – the

first delicious taste of success. Aged ten, he was standing on a chair performing a sleight-of-hand in the front room of M K Thakur. A friend of his father and amateur magician, he'd revealed the first secrets of conjuring, and taught the young Harry Singh everything he knew.

The elation of recollected success was tinged with sorrow, as he recalled how the inimitable M K Thakur had quit Blackpool for Bombay. Presenting his pupil with Houdini's literary masterpiece, *Miracle Mongers and their Methods*, he vanished from the magic-obsessed teenager's life.

The sound of a door slamming shut was followed by the sound of feet scurrying over polished linoleum. Bitu appeared backstage, his forehead gleaming with sweat.

'Get onstage, quick!' he hissed.

'Huh?'

'What's wrong with you?'

'Not feeling as right as rain,' Harry replied, befuddled.

'Go on, get through there – the bloody Americans are about to come in!'

'I can't go on with it, Bitu-bhai.'

'What?!'

'You heard me. I'm not a magician. I'm a flop.'

'No one's asking you to be a bloody magician! They don't need tricks. They need *real* magic – love, hope, joy – that kind of stuff!'

Bitu snatched the turban from Harry's hand, and furled it around his friend's head as fast as he could.

'You look *stu-bleedin'-pendous!*' he yelled.

'I'm a fake and a fraud,' Harry moaned dismally. 'And I deserve to go straight to Hell.'

Bitu grabbed his friend by the arm.

'One day we'll be laughing about this moment over a good single malt,' he roared. 'Now get out there, and remember you're not Maharaja Malipasse, but His Bloody Celestial Highness Sri Omo-ji – King of the Godmen!'

12

THE AMERICANS WERE led through into the ashram's gymnasium, in which a female instructor was demonstrating the art of 'yogic flying'.

Bouncing up and down on a trampoline, while holding the lotus position, she was transfixed in a meditative state. Decked out in matching tracksuits bearing the Sri Omo-ji logo, half a dozen students were doing their best to follow the teacher's lead.

Karnika opened a door at the far end of the gym.

'And through here is the garden,' she said, 'where we shall see the archery with meditation class.'

Traipsing behind her, the Americans ummed and ahhed at everything they saw, flabbergasted that neither their beloved Sri Omo-ji, nor His Highness the Maharaja, had mentioned the ashram before.

Six archery targets had been set up in the gardens. The devotees, who were known as *punyas*, were taking it in turns to fire at them, blindfolded.

Remarkably, three of them hit the gold.

'His Celestial Highness encourages His disciples to meditate through activities,' Karnika explained as she opened the door to the refectory. 'He believes in beauty through the unification of mind and body.'

Filing into the dining hall, the Americans watched a stream of devotees being served dinner. Rosco pointed at a magnificent stained-glass mobile suspended from the ceiling. Like almost everything else, it was adorned with the number 6 set amid a hexagon.

'That must have taken months to make,' Rosco said.

Swallowing hard, Karnika smoothed a hand back over her long black hair.

'When required, we Indians are expert at getting things done faster than fast,' she said.

13

DRIFTING THROUGH THE billowing saffron curtains into the Hall of Unconditional Love, His Celestial Highness greeted the audience with *namaste*, and slipped dreamily onto a furry white sofa in the middle of the stage.

A technician appeared from nowhere, and adjusted the microphone, before vanishing again. A pair of high-power beams bathed the godman in twin shafts of platinum light.

As Harry gazed down at the devotees – *his* devotees – a door at the back of the hall opened a crack, and the

Americans sauntered in.

'His Highness holds a nightly prayer session in here,' Karnika explained in a whisper. 'Sometimes He sits in silence, and on other evenings He speaks for hours and hours, depending on His mood.'

'It's so wonderful to see Him again,' Fred gushed.

'Just being in His presence makes me feel whole,' added Rosco.

'Could we sit and listen to the discourse for a minute or two?' Elaine asked.

Nodding, Karnika led the group to the front of the hall. Self-conscious at being so close to the guru again, the Americans sat cross-legged and peered in wonder at the illuminated stage.

Focused on the middle distance, Harry did his best to forget the audience as his magical training taught him to do. His mind blurring, he thought of growing up in the backstreets of Blackpool, and of his dad beating him for not tidying the bedroom he shared with his brother. Then he thought of the day the health inspector turned up at the butcher shop, and how his mum had cried buckets the day all the furniture had been repossessed. But most of all he thought of the pain that had shadowed his entire life, pain from hiding who he really was.

For ten long minutes Sri Omo-ji just sat there, head pounding, hands trembling in fear. A dozen times he had the first line of an oration in his mouth. But each time, something stopped him – the memory of ridicule on the last night at the Blackpool Grand.

Reclining on the furry white sofa, he saw himself reflected, as though a mirror were facing him at the edge of the stage. He was about to recoil in horror; but as his face muscles tensed to do just that, he heard a voice in his head... the voice of his first magician-teacher, M K Thakur.

'A great show is a harmony between audience and performer,' it said, 'in which each loses themselves in their role, drawing strength from one another.'

His blood fortified by a surge of adrenalin, His Celestial Highness took a deep breath, swallowed hard, and began:

'Love is wisdom and wisdom is love. Not the false love of the impure, but the love which causes roses to bloom. The love on the faces of innocent babies. The love that seeks to give but not take. The love uncounted in dollars or rupees, but rather in the communal spirit of tenderness...'

14

FOUR HOURS AND five minutes after slipping onto the furry white sofa, His Celestial Highness rose to his feet. He put both hands over his face in a curious new greeting, and drifted back through the saffron-coloured curtains, to where Bitu was waiting for him.

'How did I do?' Harry asked.

'Listen to them clapping! They loved it! And not only the Americans! The homeless people are clapping too – and none of them speak English.'

'Did I go on too long?'

Bitu's face froze.

'*No!*'

'What now?'

'You go through to the staff room and keep out of sight. I'll invite Rosco and the group to stay.'

'Stay here... at the school?'

'At the *ashram*,' Bitu corrected.

'Why?'

'Because it's the best way to reel them in!'

15

NEXT MORNING BITU woke with a start, the tail end of a nightmare coursing through his slumberous mind.

It had featured an orange laser beam shooting from the Great Stone up to the heavens, and thousands of devotees arriving from all corners of the world.

Once dressed, Bitu went out to the front of the building to inspect the stone. Across the gravel quadrangle, Karnika was at the main gate, chatting with a young man who was wearing a heavy backpack, dangling with camping accessories.

Requesting that he wait outside, she paced over to the Great Stone, where the Maharaja of Patiala was standing, his mind on orange laser beams.

'Good morning Your Highness.'

'Good morning.'

'Sir, that Canadian man over there has come to be a student of His Celestial Highness.'

Bitu looked at her askance.

'He says he saw a quote from Sri Omo-ji.'

'Where?'

'On Instagram, sir.'

'What's his name?'

'Mr Marney, Your Highness.'

'Bring him over to me.'

The security guard unlocked the gate, wrote the visitor's name on a clipboard, then Karnika led him across to where Bitu was sitting on the bench.

'Hello, I'm Marney… from Toronto,' he said brightly, thrusting out his hand to shake.

Rather affronted at being mistaken for an ordinary member of society, Bitu introduced himself as the Maharaja of Patiala. He extended his right hand to be kissed. Never having encountered royalty before, real or faux, the Canadian bent down and touched his forehead to the hand.

'You want to study under His Celestial Highness?'

'Yes, sir.'

'May I ask why?'

'Because He is Light in a World of Darkness.'

'How do you know that?'

'Because I read it on Instagram.'

'*Really?*'

'Yes, sir.'

'When?'

'Last night.'

Excellent, Bitu thought to himself, the social media guy in Shenzhen has delivered.

'Forgive me, sir,' Marney said, his voice faltering, 'but haven't we met before?'

'I certainly doubt it.'

The Canadian scratched his head.

'I'm sure we have... on the packed train to the Kumbh Mela.'

'Must have been someone who looked like me.'

His line of sight lifting, Marney's gaze fell on a huge awning hanging over the front of the main building, the image of Sri Omo-ji, and the slogan: 'His Celestial Highness Prays for the Unloved Children!'

'That's Harry,' Marney said warmly. 'He was with you on the train. Then I bumped into him at the Kumbh. We were at Mother Mee's *darshan* together.'

Swallowing hard, Bitu beckoned the Canadian to lean in.

'His Highness and I were travelling incognito,' he said quietly. 'Tell no one of meeting us – either at the Kumbh Mela, or on the way there.'

'I understand.'

Relieved, Bitu smiled.

'Tell me, what did you do before coming to India?'

'I was studying electrical engineering – graduated top of my class.'

The Maharaja signalled to Karnika to come over.

'See that Mr Marney gets breakfast, then take him to the dormitories,' he said.

'At once, Your Highness.'

The Canadian lifted his backpack from the gravel.

'By the way,' Bitu said without turning, 'd'you know anything about laser beams?'

16

BEFORE THE MORNING was out, the Americans had relocated from the Taj Ganges to the dormitories at the Sri Omo-ji Ashram.

Lavished with full VIP treatment, they were attended by an army of fawning minions. In their rooms they found a variety of key objects awaiting them, laid out neatly on their beds. These included a set of saffron-coloured robes, a framed picture of the guru to wear around their necks, a Sri Omo-ji workbook, and a pair of gloves in a pouch.

Abundantly spacious, the VIP quarters were furnished in orange upholstery, the walls festooned in proverbs and sayings uttered from His Celestial Highness's lips. The bathrooms were exceptionally luxurious, with roll-top tubs, and Italian towels. The only thing missing was a mirror above the sink. In place of it was a life-sized portrait of Sri Omo-ji, captioned with the words 'Embrace the Reflection of the Inner You'.

Changing into his robes, Rosco hung the circular photo frame around his neck, and gave thanks for the life of the guru. Before convening with the others, he washed his hands with a bar of soap engraved with the godman's image, then dried them on an orange towel embroidered with the word 'LOVE', translated into fifty languages.

Down the hall, through a door with a push-button code, Harry and Bitu were running through a list of details.

'Don't know how we're gonna stay on top of it all,' Harry said in a fluster. 'Zap's done wonders, but I'd say we're already out of our league.'

As though unfazed, Bitu swished a hand through the air.

'No problem,' he muttered. 'That girl Karnika's doing a fine job. I've green-lit a list of courses.'

'What courses?'

'Dozens of them... everything from Celestial Pottery With Meditation to Unarmed Combat in the Name of Peace.'

'D'you think she's onto us?' Harry intoned, his voice cold.

'Of course not!' Bitu jeered. 'But if anyone is it's the young Canadian chap who turned up this morning. Saw you on Instagram. Says he knows you.'

'*What?*'

'He was on the train to Allahabad – remember?'

Harry nodded.

'Yeah he was… and he took me to that nutty woman's audience… the one all dressed in white.'

'Should we chuck him out?' Bitu asked.

'No, no. Let's reach out to him… we could get him working for us.'

'I already have,' Bitu answered.

Harry tapped a clenched fist to his chin.

'The big question is how we monetize all this,' he said. 'If we don't get proper funding we'll burn out before we've even begun.'

'Need to hit Rosco P Schultz III with a wall of love,' Bitu answered. 'Imagine what a show we could lay on with some serious cash!'

'Rosco needs more than love,' Harry said. 'He needs magic!'

17

AT SUNSET KARNIKA was called out to the front gate, where half a dozen melancholic Swedes were peering in through the railings.

They explained how they'd heard about His Celestial Highness on Radio Stockholm, and dropped everything to follow the Path. The next thing they knew, they were each presented with a thirty-page contract to sign. The document had been hastily put together by the Maharaja of Patiala, copying and pasting text from a legal site online.

'What's this for?' a Swede named Marek asked.

'Just the usual legal nonsense,' Karnika responded casually.

'It looks very thorough.'

'No more than the legalese stuff you agree to when opening a Gmail account. The difference is that we print it out for you in the name of transparency.'

Marek made a joke in Swedish and his friends laughed long and hard. Then, without delay, he turned to the last page and signed.

The other Scandinavians did the same.

Karnika put her hands over her face in the greeting Sri Omo-ji had demonstrated the night before.

'Welcome to a fragment of Paradise,' she said.

At eight pm an announcement was made through miniature speakers mounted into the ceiling of every room.

Everyone was to come to the Hall of Unconditional Love at once, and to bring with them their pouch containing the rubber gloves. His Celestial Highness had a secret to reveal.

Filing in eagerly, the Americans, the Swedes, the sole Canadian, and all the homeless locals took their places – the foreigners pushing their way to the front.

'Can't wait to know what the secret is!' Elaine gushed.

'And I can't wait to find out what these gloves are for,'

Rosco said.

Marney, who'd overheard the comments, had a guess:
'Bet you they're both to do with eternal love.'

The house lights slowly dimmed, and the sound of a
sperm whale calling for a mate was played, slowed down
to half-speed. The hall was infused with the scent of
lemongrass – sprayed from ducts in the ceiling.

Fifteen minutes of absolute silence passed.

When the audience could stand the anticipation
no longer, His Celestial Highness drifted through the
curtains and onto the stage. Gliding to the front, he
stood tall, placed his hands over his face, and cried,
'*Mamana!*'

Spontaneously, the entire audience echoed the
greeting.

The godman launched into an extended monologue
about hope, energy, and 'hot love'. Having dictated so
much godspeak he found it now rolled off his tongue
effortlessly, while he thought about mundane matters,
like whether he'd have pizza or curry for a late night snack.

An hour into his oration, Sri Omo-ji paused. His face
breaking into a grin, he said:

'Those of us who hold *Mamana* in our hearts have
powers above and beyond those of mortal women and
men. We walk on this sacred planet with inner ecstasy,
and we use our powers with care.'

Staring out at the audience, twin beams of light
illuminating him, the guru reached up to his right ear,

shaped his hand into a fist and jerked it twice. A white dove fluttered into the rafters. He coughed, regurgitating another dove. After that, he threw a pair of fireballs, the flames tinged blue. And, lastly, he vanished in a puff of smoke, rematerializing at the back of the hall.

As the audience applauded in jubilation, Sri Omo-ji covered his face and exclaimed: '*Mamana!*'

Stepping up onto the stage, he slipped down onto the furry white sofa, and asked the devotees to take the gloves from their pouches and to put them on.

As soon as they did the godman explained that to know hot love they would need to feel pain.

Although ordinary on the exterior, the gloves were designed to give the wearer a taste of the anguish suffered by the Unloved Children. The right glove contained hundreds of miniature needles, while the left was laced with an irritant that made the skin burn.

'We must know pain in order to know joy,' His Celestial Highness said. 'For this reason all *punyas* must wear the Healing Gloves for three hours each day.'

Diving back into another discourse of meaningless godspeak, the spiritual leader rambled on and on. Straining to concentrate, the audience endured the discomfort of the Healing Gloves throughout.

At the end of his extended oration, the living god stood to his feet and vanished – just like that.

Where he'd been standing was a jumbled heap of saffron-orange robes.

18

OVER THE NEXT week, each day at the ashram marked a milestone.

On Monday, an orange laser beam was switched on at a special ceremony, and the nightly Ritual of the Great Stone began.

On Tuesday, Healing Socks were handed out, to complement the empathic pain of the Healing Gloves.

On Wednesday, the first printed copies of His Celestial Highness's masterwork, *The Path of Omo*, arrived.

On Thursday, a horoscope department was set up to project auspicious 'Omo-ji Moments' in the lives of every devotee.

On Friday, a $5 million donation was received from an anonymous benefactor in Silicon Valley, the funds having been channelled by Zap into a legitimate account at Citibank.

On Saturday, a competition for the best depiction of Sri Omo-ji was initiated. Chosen by His Celestial Highness himself, the winner was Rosco P Schultz III, whose blank white canvas was thought to embody the concept of 'Oneness' in a particularly propitious way.

And, on Sunday, the greatest announcement of all was made: the Seventeenth Incarnation of His Celestial Highness Omo-ji had begun. All *punyas* were instructed to exchange their saffron-coloured robes for new ones – in a vibrant shade of turquoise.

The change of colour caused disquiet among many of the followers, who'd got used to the saffron robes. A group of them asked Karnika whether they could keep the costume. Refusing, she explained how she'd received instructions from the high command. All traces of the Sixteenth Incarnation, including anything of the colour orange, was to be burned.

At dusk on the Sunday night, a monumental funeral pyre was built. All the orange robes, turbans, curtains, bed sheets, wall hangings and bath towels were thrown onto it – along with every single photo and illustration depicting His Celestial Highness's previous incarnation.

New photographs of the godman wearing turquoise were placed in frames hanging around necks, in bathrooms, bedrooms and dormitories. Every image on the website and on the social media platforms was changed, too. All the recently printed copies of *The Path of Omo* bearing the Sixteenth Incarnation portrait were incinerated, and copies of an updated edition, with the guru wearing turquoise, were handed out.

Day and night would-be *punyas* arrived, having heard about Sri Omo-ji through the slew of posts gone viral. They hastened to Varanasi by plane, train, bus, river, on bicycles, and by foot. As the social media content was translated into new languages, it reached fresh frontiers — in the Americas, Africa, Europe, Asia, and the Antipodes.

Holed up in their nerve centre, in what had once

been the school staff room, Bitu and Harry were doing their best to stay calm.

A secret surveillance system was installed. It covered every corner of the ashram – the public areas and kitchens, the gardens, dormitories, bedrooms, and even in the bathrooms.

A grid of images streamed from the video cameras was projected on a giant screen at the back of the nerve centre.

'Just bloody look at all that!' Bitu yelled.

'It's insane,' Harry said, his voice fearful and cold. 'It's like a monster, and we created it! If it carries on like this we're gonna lose control.'

'I've put Zap on a full-time salary,' Bitu answered.

'Where would we be without the fixer who can fix the unfixable?'

'In deep shit.'

Harry groaned.

'We're reaching a point where even he won't be able to save us.'

'His team are building sixty-five cabins behind the ashram.'

'Where?'

'On waste ground,' Bitu said. 'Space for another fifteen hundred *punyas*.'

'What's the total so far?'

Bitu clicked the computer's mouse.

'Last count, two thousand nine hundred and twelve.'

'Jesus Christ!'

'Remember sitting at the end of Blackpool Pier in the rain?' Bitu whispered.

Harry bit his upper lip anxiously.

'We could transfer the accounts Zap's opened for us, and tiptoe away in the night,' he said.

'They'd think it was a sign.'

'So?'

'So they'd track us down.'

'You're right,' Harry remarked in dread. 'They'd hunt us to the ends of the Earth.'

'Thought giving them a new colour to think about would take their minds off everything else,' Bitu moaned.

'The more attention we give them, the more they want.'

'So what to do?'

Harry stood up and ambled over to the screen, the collage of images projected over him.

'Sri Omo-ji will begin a period of self-imposed silence.'

Bitu grinned.

'Excellent idea! An Era of Wordlessness!' he cried.

19

THAT EVENING, WHEN the *punyas* filed into the Hall of Unconditional Love, each one was presented with a turquoise face mask.

Unfazed by the request, the fixer had sourced five

thousand of them from a medical equipment firm in Kolkata.

In an effort to be regarded as especially conscientious, many of the devotees had taken to wearing the Healing Gloves and Socks day and night. Suffering was a small price if it helped them to feel the pain of the Unloved Children.

Once they were seated, Karnika made her way to the front, clipboard in hand. Stepping up onto the stage, she made her way to the microphone and greeted the turquoise-clad congregation.

'*Mamana!*' she cried, hands placed over her face, as Sri Omo-ji had taught them all to do.

Animated by a sense of fresh anticipation, the devotees returned the greeting so loudly that the hall's floor shook.

'*Mamana!*'

Karnika held up the clipboard, signalling an official announcement was about to be made.

'I have an important message,' she said gravely.

Drawn from all corners of the world, and unified in their love for Sri Omo-ji, the audience listened anxiously.

'From this moment,' Karnika said, reading from the clipboard, 'His Celestial Highness Sri Omo-ji will begin a period of silence, in honour of those with no voices. "The Era of Wordlessness" has begun. In respect for this sacred act of devotion, we humbly request *punyas* to do the same.'

Taking out a turquoise surgical mask, Karnika mouthed the word '*Mamana*', pulled the straps over her ears, and quit the stage.

Within a minute everyone in the Hall of Unconditional Love had copied her, donning their masks, and joining their guru in the Era of Wordlessness.

20

EACH EVENING, SRI Omo-ji would sit on the stage in the furry white chair, his mouth hidden by the mask, fingers woven together on his lap.

Cross-legged and obedient below him, the devotees would wait stock-still in silence, surgical masks in place. Some of them closed their eyes; others stared at the stage or into the middle distance. Yet more wept uncontrollably, their sobs muffled out of respect for the Era of Wordlessness.

Four times a week, Bitu and Harry would meet in the staff room and make lists of new courses to hold, traditions to start, and bizarre symbols to adopt. They scoped out plans for elaborate media projects, too, as well as eccentricities and whims – the kind which made Sri Omo-ji seem all the more alluring.

With thousands of *punyas* now installed at the ashram, it was decided at one such meeting to allocate a scale of superiority among the devotees, numbering them in the order they arrived at the ashram. The first five numbers were not given to people but to the senses

– sight, sound, smell, touch, and taste.

The godman was number 6, the most sacred number of all.

Number 7 was the Maharaja of Patiala. As deputy, he was the only person permitted to address Sri Omo-ji. Rosco and the original group of Americans took numbers after that, as did Zap the fixer, Karnika, Marney, and the Swedes. Forming the inner circle, they were responsible for the running of the ashram, and for implementing the divine plans set out by His Celestial Highness.

The elite devotees regarded themselves as superior to rank-and-file *punyas* because of their proximity to Sri Omo-ji. They took to wearing a turquoise ribbon around their wrists – evidence of their elevated standing. As it happened, the symbol of the ribbon came about by chance. The godman had been sent three-dozen boxes of Swiss chocolates from a well-wisher in Zurich. Fearing the confectionaries might be laced with poison, Bitu passed them out at a staff meeting. As a joke, Elaine had tied the turquoise ribbon from the box around her wrist. Not to be outdone, the others copied her, and a status symbol was born.

During the time of silence, members of the ashram became used to communicating through sign language. For more complicated matters, they used notes written on little turquoise pads, which were suspended around their necks, along with the photo and the garlands.

Although not especially keen on the silence, *punyas* went along with it because His Celestial Highness had ordered them not to speak.

Brought in to bump up the original numbers, the homeless devotees were the only ones who enjoyed the Wordlessness – as they didn't understand any English at all.

Three months after The Era of Wordlessness began, Sri Omo-ji was sitting in silence on the furry sofa, the sea of devotees below the stage wearing turquoise face masks. The nightly orations had been hard work, but the guru missed them, and was regretting announcing the self-imposed silence. Sitting there on the stage, he pined for the days of his previous career, as a stage magician.

An idea took seed.

Before Harry knew it, he'd come up with a full plan – a plan to liven things up, and get everyone back in the groove. Getting to his feet, he stepped up to the microphone at the edge of the stage, and tapped it twice.

Then, in an action that was to go down in Sri Omo-ji folklore, he removed his face mask and decreed:

'The Era of Miracles has begun!'

21

THE DAY AFTER the announcement, Karnika was welcoming a group of newly arrived Korean followers at the main gate, when she noticed a brand new SUV parked across the street.

The windows were blacked out, and the number plate unmistakably registered to the Government of India. Karnika was about to dismiss the vehicle as unimportant, when she spotted a small camera mounted at the top of the front passenger door. Checking with the guards, she learned that it had been parked in the very same spot for more than a week.

Like all A-list celebrities, godmen across India were targets of maniacs and extremists – a point that concerned the ashram's elite increasingly.

From the second month onwards, would-be *punyas* were expected to go through airport-style security on arrival, as well as a brief interview and background check – all in addition to signing the standard agreement to abide by the ashram's rules.

The week before the arrival of the government vehicle, a small security incident had taken place at the ashram. A newly arrived devotee from Hyderabad had been seen with a homemade machete. On examination, his luggage was found to contain hand-drawn map of the ashram, and notes on the guru's schedule.

The incident had led to a new range of safety measures.

Passport scans were taken, before being emailed to an independent verification unit near London. Anyone who seemed suspect was thanked for their interest in Sri Omo-ji but politely refused entry.

Having made it past the security stage, and after

signing the agreement consisting of small-print legalese, the Koreans were ushered to the Great Stone. The group had seen pictures of the sacred monument online, and were all greatly moved to now be standing before it in person.

One-by-one they were shown how to circumambulate it backwards six times. Only when they had performed this perfectly, were they permitted to enter the main part of the ashram.

By late afternoon, the Koreans were dressed in their turquoise robes, framed photos of the godman dangling from their necks. They were invited to sign up for the courses on offer – almost all of which featured meditation, self-reflection, and chanting the central mantra '*Mamana*'.

The latest arrivals were then led through a central courtyard, presented with a translation of *The Path of Omo* in Korean, and asked to clear their minds of anything and everything they'd ever known. They were no longer to worry about the trials and tribulations of their lives, but to prepare themselves to embrace the joy of joys – the Love and Peace of His Celestial Highness Sri Omo-ji.

22

AT THE MORNING meeting, when the usual order of business had been cleared, Bitu looked at his friend and winced.

'*Era of Miracles*?' he said disapprovingly.

'Thought it was time to shake things up a bit,' Harry replied. 'All that silence was getting to me.'

'It was getting to everyone, but it was wonderful for the balance sheet,' Bitu countered. '*Crores* and *crores* are coming in every day through donations on the site.'

'There's a lesson in it somewhere,' Harry answered. 'Tell people they can't speak and they open their wallets all the more.'

He glanced at the spreadsheet.

'Look at it – most of the donations came from people outside India.'

'Yes, but the virtual followers loved the silence.'

'That's friggin' insane.'

'They were unified in the mysterious silent power of Sri Omo-ji!' Bitu giggled.

'Time for a new direction,' Harry said. 'I'll do a nightly show. I'll prove to them that I'm a living god.'

'What d'you have in mind?'

'Some of the feats from the old stage show.'

'Don't you think it's better to keep it light?'

Harry stepped over to the mirror and looked at himself.

'This is crazy, Bitu-bhai! Look what I've become!'

'A living god,' his friend replied caustically. 'Just what you always dreamed of.'

Harry's smile melted.

'No...' he answered heatedly. 'I dreamed of being the best stage magician in the world!'

'But this is so much bigger than that.'

'Bigger isn't necessarily better.'

'Harry-bhai, look at yourself!' Bitu said. 'How many people can say that they became a god in human form?'

'I'm not a god – and we both know it.'

'Fine – but you're worshipped as one, which is even better!'

Harry's expression darkened.

'If only the clasp hadn't seized in the Blackpool Grand that night,' he said dismally, 'the whole course of my life would have been different.'

Bitu groaned.

'Believe that if you like!' he yelled. 'But you'd be on the bloody magician's scrap heap by now – you know it as well as me. This though is your destiny!'

Walking over to the far wall, on which the security camera grid was projected, Bitu stooped to pick something up... a shoebox.

In silence he took it over to where Harry was sitting.

'Know what's in here?'

'Nope.'

Bitu rolled his eyes.

'What d'you see?' he asked, opening it.

Harry rummaged through the contents.

'Some used cotton buds, wet wipes, dental floss, and an empty tube of toothpaste... a lot of rubbish,' he said, frowning.

'It may be to you – and to me... but to everyone out

there it's treasure.'

'*Huh?*'

'I found the *punyas* fighting over it all last night – relics discarded by their Lord and Master, the great Sri Omo-ji.'

'That's insane!'

'It may be,' Bitu answered. 'But it's true.'

23

ON THE FIRST night of the Era of Miracles, His Celestial Highness gave a three-hour oration – not seated on the furry white sofa but apparently levitating three feet in the air.

The second night, he cloned himself to produce five holographic copies of himself, and delivered his address through all six of them. Next evening, he was lowered into a vat of turquoise liquid, before miraculously appearing unscathed at the back of the hall. The night after that, fifty devotees were selected at random. Blindfolded, they uttered a single word out loud – '*Mamana*', at which Sri Omo-ji correctly identified them by name, and gave their passport number and place of birth.

The greatest miracle was kept for the fifth night.

An hour before it was to take place, Karnika announced through the public address system that everyone was to sit on the floor wherever they were and pray for the soul of His Celestial Highness. They were to chant '*Mamana!*' over and over, and think of a turquoise river wending its way through valleys and down to the sea.

At the appointed moment, Karnika revealed that the miracle wasn't going to take place in the Hall of Unconditional Love, but outside in the gardens.

Ten minutes after that, every single devotee arrived in the orchard, between the main ashram buildings and the orderly rows of log cabins. Milling about, they wondered aloud what the miracle might be.

After a short delay, Marney called for three volunteers. Everyone begged to be chosen.

Selecting three burly Russians who'd arrived the week before from Vladivostok, Marney gave them each a spade and asked them to dig a grave in the shade of the apple trees.

At seeing the grave take shape, a sense of panic swept through the devotees. Dozens of them fell on the grass and began wailing, tearing out their hair, lamenting that their beloved Sri Omo-ji had gone.

Once the grave was six feet deep, a stream of *punyas* hurried forward, wooden buckets of turquoise rose petals in their hands. With their fellow disciples looking on, they scattered handfuls of petals into the grave, until the hole was neatly blanketed in a soft bed of turquoise.

Then, a magnificent casket was borne forward, carried by the six Swedes from the inner circle, Marek pacing sombrely before them. Crafted from polished teak, and adorned with the number six, the coffin was lowered to the ground, and sprinkled in yet more rose petals.

After a pause for reflection, Rosco and the other trusted Americans pushed their way to the front. On bended knees they leant down and kissed the casket. When they had done so, the other devotees lined up to do the same – assuming it was part of a mysterious new ritual.

From the comfort of the staff room, the Maharaja of Patiala and the godman watched the screen filled with a view of the grave.

'Looks like they're ready for me,' Harry said.

'I've got a bad feeling about this,' Bitu said. 'Let's call it off.'

'No way! I've wanted to do a human hibernation since I was a kid. Thakur said a *sadhu* called Haridas had performed it in the 1830s. It's a thing of magical legend.'

Bitu grunted in protest.

'That's all well and good, but did he have a bandwagon like this to keep going while he was six feet under?'

Harry didn't answer.

He took a turquoise turban from the back of the chair, wound the full length around his head, and looked at himself in the mirror – the only one in the entire ashram. Pulling a face, he glided outside into the orchard.

The devotees' spirits were instantly buoyed at seeing the guru.

Ten *punyas* from Rio de Janeiro prostrated themselves on the grass. A minute later, everyone was doing the same. His forehead beading in sweat, Sri Omo-ji whispered an instruction to Marney.

Then, in silence he stepped into the coffin and lay down.

The atmosphere was electric, as though something tremendously significant was about to take place. The Brazilians, who'd started the craze of prostrating themselves to His Celestial Highness, lurched forwards and begged to be buried in the godman's place.

Calmly, Marney asked them to step back, which they did. And, just as he'd been told to do, he knelt down, and held Sri Omo-ji's wrist.

Alarmed, he turned to the devotees.

'There's no pulse,' he said.

The Brazilians, Russians, Swedes, and at least half the Koreans wept uncontrollably. Some tore branches from the trees and beat themselves. The Americans were more sanguine. Rosco covered his face with his hands and gave blessings for the short but extraordinary Seventeenth Incarnation. Like everyone else, he was speechless that the guru had slipped away before their eyes.

Marney was the only one who remained completely calm.

'If you don't trust me,' he said in a firm voice, 'trust our beloved Sri Omo-ji. Before His soul slipped away, He whispered a promise to me.'

'What did He say?!' someone screeched.

'Tell us! Tell us!' chanted a frantic chorus.

'He said that He was merely going to sleep.'

'For how long?!'

'For as long as a crop of carrots takes to grow.'

24

ONCE THE CASKET'S lid had been screwed into place and the box had been lowered down into the grave, the *punyas* whipped up hysterically again.

Howling with sorrow, some took fists of turquoise petals and scattered them down onto the coffin.

Little by little the hole was filled in with earth.

The topsoil was raked flat, and a crop of seeds was planted and watered. A pair of copper timpani was carried to the side of the grave, and two Bulgarian disciples began striking them in a slow, rhythmic beat.

Hundreds of devotees stayed at the graveside until the middle of the night. The thought of Sri Omo-ji being buried was too much for many to bear.

Night and day, the kettledrums were struck, reminding the *punyas* that His Celestial Highness was six feet under. As they kept retelling each other, he was performing an act of selfless love and peace for them, and for the Unloved Children.

A week passed and the drumming didn't stop for a moment. Proving themselves to be first-rate drummers, the Bulgarians shared the task between themselves, taking it in shifts to mark the passage of time.

During the day the devotees would pause from their

classes or their duties and drift out to sit beside the grave in silence. A few of them slept out in the garden, and refused to ever leave.

Within a few days the first shoots pushed through and, by the second week, they had turned into luxuriant tufts of green. The inner-circle Americans took charge of watering the crop, measuring out the exact amount of purified water necessary – the liquid having been blessed each morning at the Great Stone.

25

AT THE END of the second week, three slate-grey vans screeched to a halt at the ashram's gates and a horde of uniformed police leapt out.

They were led by an officer whose name badge read 'G G Gambhir'. Waving a certified document triumphantly above his head, he demanded to be permitted entry. As he remonstrated, a pair of police trucks rolled up. Amid billowing exhaust fumes dozens of extra officers clambered out.

Having expected a police raid for weeks, Zap the fixer had given the devotees regular briefings, and forced them to memorize ten key rules:

1. No one is to tell anyone outside the ashram about the goings-on inside.
2. Anyone suspecting they are being followed is to report it immediately.
3. Any drones flying above the ashram are to be shot

out of the sky.

4. Buildings and streets in the surrounding area are to be watched round the clock for unusual activity.

5. The auxiliary power unit is to be tested twice a week, and emergency drills are to be practised every other day.

6. No devotee is permitted to reveal 'Sri Omo-ji Secrets' (specific code words given to each poonya each week, and checked for on social media by Two-See in Shenzhen).

7. Anyone caught taking relics discarded by Sri Omo-ji is to be publicly disgraced.

8. No one is to speak to His Celestial Highness directly unless invited to do so.

9. No drugs, hard liquor, or pornography of any kind is permitted at the ashram.

10. On no account is anyone to ever communicate with the police, secret service, or any other official.

Karnika was called out to the front gate, where she did her best to appease the ranting and raving of the chief officer, G G Gambhir.

'You cannot stop us gaining entry and making a full inspection!' he bawled, flapping the legal document at her.

The tirade was transmitted to the administration office by way of a miniature lapel camera and microphone below Karnika's right shoulder. Clustered around a computer screen, the inner circle discussed what to do.

'Our lawyers will kick them into the long grass!' yelled Rosco.

'They've got no right to come in here!' Marek added.

Zap grabbed a desktop microphone, linked to Karnika's earpiece.

'Open the gates and let them in,' he said, 'we have nothing to hide!'

The instruction was relayed to the guards, who unlocked the gates.

A minute later, at least a hundred police officers surged into the compound.

At the vanguard, like a general leading his army into battle, was G G Gambhir.

Suspicious and scathing, he made a beeline for the Great Stone. In the shadow of the sacred rock a group of devotees who'd just arrived from Paraguay were performing the backwards circumambulation. Each of them was wailing like an Arctic wolf howling at the moon.

'What's all this?!' the chief officer bellowed.

'A ritual in honour of His Celestial Highness Sri Omo-ji,' Karnika replied.

'What's that laser for?'

'A symbol of peace and love.'

Huffing and puffing, Gambhir hurried forward, pushing through double doors into the main building. Close behind Karnika, the droves of uniformed officers followed.

Against the muffled booming of the timpani, the police spread out. They'd been briefed to make notes on anything that seemed out of the ordinary. Even for India, where the unusual *is* usual, almost everything they witnessed was out of the ordinary.

In the kitchens, the police found the chefs praying over six sprigs of rosemary. When asked why, they answered that the herb was a favourite of Sri Omo-ji – and that all rosemary was honoured with a *puja* before it was cooked. Other ingredients blessed with devotion included carrots, pinto beans, and cream cheese.

In the gymnasium, a posse of officers burst into the so-called 'Mania Zone'. Three hundred and twelve *punyas* were packed inside. Amid the pulsating laser light, they gyrated about, screaming in complete silence.

Another hall, the 'Rumi Room', was occupied by seventy devotees spinning round and round like whirling dervishes. When quizzed on what they were doing, the *punyas* fell to the floor and laughed hysterically.

Breaking out of the main cluster of buildings, G G Gambhir stormed through the gardens where all manner of meditative activities were taking place, Karnika on his heels.

Wherever he looked, Sri Omo-ji's followers were meditating in the shade or strolling between the trees, all of them with ear-to-ear grins. When greeting one another, they would hug as though embracing a long-lost friend.

Heatedly, the officer turned to face Karnika.

'Where is he?!'

'Where's who, sir?'

'The damned Omo.'

'Respectfully, sir, we do not speak of Him in that way… we refer to His Celestial Highness, or "Sri Omo-ji".'

'All right… where is your Omo-ji?!'

Karnika shrugged.

'Unavailable,' she said.

'Is that so, miss…? Well would you inform me when he will be available?!'

'I am not absolutely certain.'

'Why not?'

'Because,' Karnika responded, 'I am not sure how long carrots take to grow.'

26

NINETY-THREE FEET below the Hall of Unconditional Love lay a secure zone, strictly off limits to even the inner circle.

The secret bunker had been paid for by an especially large anonymous donation from Greece. Zap had sourced a Swiss firm to handle the construction, ordering the designers to build it with a beehive's hexagonal pods. Typically entrusted with secret jobs for world governments, the Swiss company was expert in high-level security. Only a handful of the inner circle knew about the safe zone, which was only ever referred to as 'the Pantry'.

Reached by an express lift, the unit was secured by a series of Durasteel blast doors. The twenty-foot concrete casing was designed to shelter those inside during a full-scale military attack – whether it be ballistic, chemical, or nuclear. Autonomous power supplies and air filtration systems meant the unit could be sealed off for months, or even years, on end.

The Pantry consisted of a warren of apartments and meeting rooms, communication and logistics hubs, personnel quarters, kitchens, supply and provision stores, and armouries. Worthy of a James Bond villain's lair, it was fully fortified.

The largest hexagonal room of all was devoted to a Cray CS Series Supercomputer, cooled round the clock by an autonomous ventilation system. Armed with the latest in artificial intelligence and deep learning capability, it crunched numbers 24/7. As a result of the computer's digital muscle, the ashram's vast share and stock portfolio gained a slight edge over other investors.

The Cray CS was one of many things sourced by the celebrated fixer. The computer had arrived from Seattle with a team of technicians charged to manage it. Forbidden entry into the main ashram at ground level, they stayed in the Pantry for two-week shifts, coming and going through the escape tunnel.

The principal armoury was stocked for a full-on assault. Among the munitions, there were three-dozen M26 fragmentation grenades, thirty M4A1 carbines, two racks of Brügger & Thomet MP9 machine pistols, a pair of Browning M2HB machine guns, as well as a full complement of tear and VX gas, and M84 stun grenades.

At the furthest end of the Pantry's central meeting room was an ordinary-looking steel cupboard, the kind used for office files. Beyond, behind a blast door, was Sri Omo-ji's personal survival suite.

A back wall was covered by a matrix of computer monitors relaying what was happening high above at ground level.

One of the screens was streaming Karnika's bodycam, while another followed the irate police chief as he thundered through the campus. A third was trained on the grave. Beside it, shirtless and drenched in perspiration, six hefty Bulgarians were pounding kettle-drums.

'He's a bloody dick!' snapped Bitu, sipping a cup of piping hot tea.

'Not as much of a dick as Rosco! Look at him – he's out there prostrating himself at *my* grave!' Harry breathed in deep, before exhaling in a long sigh, his face bearded. 'You just couldn't make this up,' he said.

Bitu let out a shrill giggle.

'The carrots are coming on nicely. I'd say you've got another month in here.'

'Only a month?' Harry countered caustically.

'Well, it was your idea – to give them a miracle of miracles.'

'Might slip out for a while. I hear Nice is nice at this time of year.'

'I've got a bad feeling,' Bitu said, failing to react to the pun. 'It's gnawing away at me down in my guts.'

'I've got it too… have had it for weeks,' Harry said.

Bitu jabbed a hand at the police chief.

'That clown up there hasn't found anything so he's going to feel humiliated.'

'Which means he'll be back.'

'To plant drugs, or to arrest us for treason?'

'Perhaps. Or with another court order… but to shut us down.'

Harry sniffed.

'Anyone tried paying off the chief?'

'Of course. But he's not interested.'

'What about framing him before he frames us?'

Bitu drained his cup.

'Do that and there'll just be another raid next month. Then another… and another.'

'So what's the answer?'

'Jump before we're pushed.'

'Are you crazy? Move all of this?!' Harry yelled.

'It's not as if we haven't got manpower. At last count we had eight thousand people up there – crammed into a school built for eight hundred spotty boys. Plus there's another twenty-five thousand would-be *punyas* signed up online.'

Harry didn't reply. Standing up, he stepped over to

his friend and looked him hard in the eye.

'Time to take the Eighteenth Incarnation somewhere else,' he said.

Bitu frowned.

'But where would we go?'

'Anywhere we like.'

'The US… Brazil… Australia?'

Sri Omo-ji pressed his fingertips together as if in prayer.

'Let's go home,' he said.

PART IV

1

Six weeks after the burial had taken place, the carrot tops were leafy and lush, and were tended as lovingly as ever by the inner circle.

At the graveside the Bulgarians were still drumming, as they had done night and day since the godman had been interred. The sound of timpani was hard-wired into everyone's heads.

It would have been inaccurate to say that anyone had forgotten His Celestial Highness Sri Omo-ji. On the contrary, he was in the thoughts and prayers of many thousands of *punyas* in Varanasi, a multitude of followers around the world, not to mention the droves of media camped outside the ashram gates.

During the final week of the so-called 'hibernation', a wave of mania tore through the ashram. Different from the usual febrile high spirits, it was characterized by something Marney later described as 'Divine Turmoil'.

The first sign of it appeared in the form of 'grouping'. Unable to bear the pain of Sri Omo-ji's absence, some devotees sewed the wrists of their turquoise robes together, forcing them to go around in pairs or clusters of three. The practice developed when a couple of *punyas* had the idea of linking their nose rings together by a short chain. Within days, hundreds of devotees were either tied or chained together in mini groups.

The second example of Divine Turmoil was the practice of what became known as 'scarring'. A devotee would take a sharpened stick and chisel a large 'O' into the back of another. If this was performed correctly, the wound scarred in little bumps.

But without doubt the oddest manifestation of communal agitation came when a devotee from Albania grabbed a steak knife in the dining hall. Yelling, 'In the name of Omo-ji!' he severed the outer part of his left ear.

Within a day, a hundred and fifty devotees had copied the act. By the middle of the week, more than a thousand *punyas* were missing either one or both of their ears. Once the blood had been cleaned off, the little tokens of devotion were carried to the grave, and placed in a pile beside where the carrots were almost full-grown.

Alarmed at the extreme manifestations of hysteria, Bitu begged his friend to cease the pointless hibernation before someone died. Heavily bearded, Harry was virtually unrecognizable from the godman who'd stepped into the casket. Indeed, he looked so different that he was able to do what he had joked of doing.

One morning shortly after dawn, armed with a brand new Slovakian passport supplied courtesy of Zap, he boarded a chartered Gulfstream. By sunset he was checking into the fabulously opulent Montserrat Caballé Suite at the Hotel Negresco in Nice.

Sipping a piña colada at the pool, dressed in a t-shirt and shorts like everyone else, he looked like any other well-heeled hipster – rather than a godman on holiday on the French Riviera.

2

OVER PREVIOUS DAYS and weeks G G Gambhir may have left the ashram alone, but it was still the one and only thing on his mind. Having gone up the chain of command, the officer had secured additional funding from the chief minister himself, in the name of national security.

Hundreds of officers were put on the case of digging up dirt on Sri Omo-ji and his followers. It wasn't long before the fixer who could fix the unfixable was in the crosshairs of Gambhir's sights.

While the majority of the devotees tended to stay within the ashram's perimeter, the fixer came and went. A lone wolf par excellence, he was charged with establishing high-level contacts as well as sourcing everything the guru needed or wanted, from guacamole to grenades.

When not at the ashram, Zap spent most of his time in a ramshackle office across from the Mutton Meat Shop on Kassab Mohal Road. A windowless room lit by bare bulbs, the walls were plastered with pictures of Zap's one and only obsession – Dolly Parton.

Late one night the fixer was leaning back on the room's single chair, talking to a canned-cheese broker in Dubai, when there was a knock at the door.

Zap frowned.

No one knew he was there.

So he didn't answer.

The knock came again, much harder.

A minute later he'd slid the bolt away, and G G Gambhir was standing in the frame.

'What d'you want?' Zap asked angrily.

'Information,' the officer replied.

'Why don't you use Google like everyone else?'

Gambhir stepped over the threshold, his eyes adjusting to the dimness. Heavyset with clumsy features and a salt and pepper moustache, he smelled of fried onions.

'In coming to you I have ventured to the horse's mouth,' he said, pleased with himself at the remark.

'Unless you haven't noticed, I don't have four legs and a tail,' the fixer replied.

'But you do have the information I'm after. And I'm not leaving here without it.'

Slipping his phone into his shirt pocket, Zap went back to his desk and sat down, leaving the officer standing.

'Call me old fashioned,' he said, 'but I believe in introductions. You seem to know who I am, so would you mind telling me who you are?'

'Officer Gambhir from Police Headquarters, Lucknow.'

Zap grinned.

'I'm flattered you think so highly of me that you'd track me down.'

The officer approached.

His breathing was strained as it always was in anger.

'Tell me who he is and where he came from!' he barked.

'*He?*'

'That wretched guru you and all the others are following.'

'You mean His Celestial…?'

Gambhir slammed a fist down on the desk, his face darkening.

'He's a damned Britisher – you know it as well as me.'

'What does it matter where he's from?' Zap shot back.

The officer changed tack.

'It doesn't,' he said softly. 'But if I don't find out, something terrible might happen. Those nice sons of yours may find themselves arrested, and that house where they live with their mother could catch fire.'

Zap the fixer stood up, his eyes burning into those of the officer.

'You haven't understood, have you?' he said. 'Sri Omo-ji isn't about a man's identity any longer. It's become far bigger than that. It's not about him, but about his essence. The essence of Peace and Love.'

G G Gambhir seethed.

'Cooperate with my investigation or get ready for your family to taste my rage!'

Calmly, Zap slipped the phone from his shirt pocket, sent the recorded conversation to a secure server, and grinned again.

'Checkmate,' he said.

3

ON THE SEVENTY-FIRST day since Sri Omo-ji's burial, an announcement was made over the ashram's speaker system:

'Time for the carrots to be picked!'

Frenziedly, the *punyas* streamed to the orchard from the main buildings, and from the rows of log cabins, and from the Great Stone, whooping and hollering as they came.

The inner circle were already standing at the graveside, a few of them holding baskets, the timpani still marking the passing of time. As the full complement of devotees watched, the carrots were eased out of the soil ceremoniously. Having been doted over for many weeks, they were quite magnificent. Cut up into little pieces, the carrots were passed around as though they were a sacrament.

Then, it was time to excavate the casket.

As the timpani were struck harder and harder, a handful of the devotees dug as though their lives depended on it. Some of the disciples who'd sacrificed their ears threw themselves on the ground, writhing about as though possessed.

All of a sudden one of the shovels struck wood.

Carefully, the diggers quarried away the last buckets of earth. The casket itself was raised, and placed gently on the grass, amid chanting, more whooping, and the ear-splitting drumming of timpani.

Half a dozen *punyas* raced forwards, electric screwdrivers in hand.

A minute later, the coffin's lid was lifted away.

Holding their breath, and in absolute silence, eight thousand disciples watched.

All over the world, tens of thousands more did the same – glued to smartphones and computer screens.

Splendidly serene, and handsomely bearded, Omo-ji was lying outstretched and apparently lifeless.

Lurching urgently forwards, Rosco felt for a pulse.

There wasn't one.

The drummers ceased.

Falling back, the American broke down inconsolably while all around him the *punyas* did the same.

Sequestered away in the former staff room, Bitu watched the live video feed. He was the only person to share in the godman's secret.

Very slowly, the fingers on Sri Omo-ji's right hand began to tremble ever so slightly. Radiating out, the faint movement progressed up his arm, and into his chest.

Marney clasped his cheeks and screamed:

'He's alive! Our beloved Master is alive!'

4

THE ASHRAM ERUPTED into celebration, the *punyas* giving thanks to the powers of the universe for watching over His Celestial Highness during his long hibernation.

Festivities continued through days and nights.

Devotees who'd sewn or chained themselves together, were unattached amid prayers of thanks. Those who'd had their backs chiselled with the letter 'O', had their wounds tended to. And those who had cut off one ear – or both – were given special duties befitting their personal sacrifice.

Meanwhile, Sri Omo-ji was left alone to recover from his ordeal. Weakened and unable to speak, he was seen praying in the orchard each afternoon, observed from a distance by almost everyone.

A week after the godman was exhumed, Zap was instructed by the Maharaja of Patiala to prepare for another colour change.

The Eighteenth Incarnation was to be emerald green.

An official photograph was taken and made ready for the circular frames. Fresh hangings were ordered, new copies of *The Path of Omo* were printed, and thousands of robes were prepared in every imaginable size.

Eight days after the end of the hibernation, a special *darshan* was called in the Hall of Unconditional Love. The *punyas* were requested to scrub themselves extra well with pumice, and to take it in turns to perform the ritual at the Great Stone.

Streaming into the Hall of Unconditional Love, the disciples were in high spirits, the trauma of the hibernation behind them. When all eight thousand three hundred and twelve devotees were in attendance, Sri Omo-ji glided through the curtains and onto the stage.

The audience went wild.

Dancing and clapping, cheering and gyrating, they were united in ecstatic bliss. Holding both hands over his face, the godman greeted his followers with '*Mamana*', the sacred word echoing back at him in a deafening chorus of supreme and consummate joy.

A minute or two passed while Sri Omo-ji took his place on the white sofa. Then, in his own time, the guru held up a hand, signalling for quiet.

Instantly, silence prevailed.

Breathing in as if still weak, Omo-ji addressed his disciples.

'I am you and you are me... our spirits are one and the same,' he said. 'Not Yin and Yang, but perfect clones of one another – pulses of electricity... atoms arranged in strings of twisting DNA. Our journey through this life is but a single phase of our own personal moon. A fleeting configuration – a breath of wind on a mountain plain.'

Cross-legged and straight-backed, the *punyas* listened more intently than any had listened before. They listened as His Celestial Highness spoke of vermilion energy, pink truth and of grey love. After the main sermon, they listened as four important announcements were made:

One: everyone was to be baptized – not in the name of a church, but in the name of something far greater:

The Power of Sacrosanct Truth.

Two: in honour of their baptism, everyone in the

audience was to have their head shaved.

Three: each *poonya* was to be given a new name.

Four: Sri Omo-ji was to assume his Eighteenth Incarnation.

A tremendous flash ripped through the hall like a lightning strike. Rubbing their eyes, the devotees focused on their leader, his robes having changed miraculously to a bright shade of emerald green.

Processing up onto the stage, the disciples were blessed by the guru. Whispering a secret incantation into the ear – or where the ear had been – he blessed each *poonya* with a few drops of sacred water.

One-by-one, the baptized devotees knelt on the floor as if about to be beheaded, and their hair was shaven expertly with a cut-throat razor – by a team of barbers sourced by the fixer at the Venkateswara Temple in Tirupati.

After that, everyone's birth name was discarded and a fresh one was bestowed with blessings and love.

Then, amid a great fanfare, the initiates stripped naked, spun round three times, and donned their new emerald-green robes.

5

ON THE FIRST full day of Sri Omo-ji's Eighteenth Incarnation, Marney was dispatched to England on a secret mission – to locate a country estate with plenty of land.

Late in the afternoon of the same day, an Indian government helicopter circled over the ashram taking photos, and scanning the buildings with thermographic cameras.

The day after, Uttar Pradesh's chief minister turned up at the gates along with his entourage. As before, when the police had arrived, Karnika was sent out to charm him. Welcomed in with open arms, he was given a tour, and even asked if he wanted to pray at the Great Stone.

'I'm afraid I don't join cults,' he'd riposted.

'We are no more a cult than it is to be a member of Netflix,' Karnika had shot back, thinking on her feet.

The chief minister was presented with a copy of *The Path of Omo* bound in emerald-green lizard skin, and with a photo of the guru in a solid gold frame. Every member of the minister's forty-strong entourage was given a limited-edition Rolex bearing the smiling face of Sri Omo-ji on the dial.

Before leaving, the minister beckoned Karnika close.

'You can tell your guru he's brought shame on Uttar Pradesh,' he growled. 'The last grains of sand are about to tumble from the hourglass!'

6

Six days after leaving for London, Marney sent an encoded message to Bitu.

It read: 'MANANA GREEN IS GO'.

'Did he send any pictures?' Harry asked at the

morning meeting.

Bitu clicked his tongue.

'Not yet.'

'Any idea where it is?'

'Nope.'

'Does it have one route in and another one out?'

'I don't bloody know, OK?!' Bitu snapped.

Harry looked at his friend, piqued at his outburst.

'Why so tetchy?'

'It's that bloody chief minister. I can feel him watching us from every angle. They've probably bugged the whole place – even in here.'

Harry frowned in a vacant kind of way.

'Think they'll attack?'

'Dunno. But I'll get Zap onto fixing documents for the homeless guys. Said he could get them Slovakian passports cheap.'

'D'you think it's best to slip away little by little?'

Bitu balked at the question.

'Half of India's secret service is camped outside the bloody gates,' he said. 'Not even Houdini could have sneaked eight thousand nutters dressed in green out of here!'

Harry glared at his old friend, as if affronted.

'Forget friggin' David Copperfield!' he quipped. 'There's only one person who could pull off a stunt like that!'

'And who might that be?'

'His Celestial Highness Sri Omo-ji of course!'

7

BEFORE LEAVING FOR England, Marney had been given a cover story and strict instructions to remain as inconspicuous as possible.

The last thing needed was for the Indian authorities to get wind that plans to move out were afoot. At the same time, Bitu and Harry feared the British government would block a property sale were they to hear it was for Sri Omo-ji's new ashram.

While waiting for his flight at Kolkata's Dum Dum Airport, Marney shortlisted possible estates, sending messages to the agents from a nondescript Gmail account.

Attired in an emerald Harris Tweed suit and matching green Hunter wellies, he was unshaven. Like almost all the godman's male followers, he had vowed to grow a beard as part of the ritual to welcome in the Eighteenth Incarnation.

Marney began by looking at several vast country estates on the Scottish Borders. Each boasted a huge country house, a working farm, a river, and forests. But however hard Marney tried, he couldn't picture Sri Omo-ji being happy in such a windswept landscape.

Driving further south in his bright green rental car, he toured a hulking stately home near the Norfolk Broads, the countryside even more bleak than in the borderlands. After five days of traipsing around dilapidated homes being hawked by impoverished aristocrats, he spotted a posting for a house in Dorset, on the banks of the River Stour. It was called Pimperne Hall, and was on the market for eleven million pounds.

Next day, dressed to the nines in his country squire get-up, Marney drove down south to take a closer look. He was pretending to be an Anglophile who had tired of the fast-paced world of Toronto's high finance. Having made a fortune, he was ready to settle down with his wife, many children, and dogs. A hunter and a fisherman, his lifelong passion was to be a gentleman – for which he needed a vast amount of land.

Following the GPS directions, Marney steered the Java-green Audi through an imposing stone gateway adorned with an ancient family crest. Beyond it lay a magnificent private drive, edged on either side by a sea of rhododendrons.

Snaking through the property for almost three miles, the approach took in a lake, an oak forest with peacocks, and a magnificent maze. As the rental car took the final bend, the house came into view like an apparition.

Monumental in grandeur and size, Pimperne Hall was a classic Georgian country pile built in 1782 on a fortune made from Caribbean sugar plantations. Greatly expanded a century later, the house had boasted a number of important owners, including two dukes and five lords – but never a living god.

Donning his tweed flat cap, Marney stepped out of

the vehicle onto the gravel.

An impeccably dressed estate agent with a double-barrelled name and an expensively produced business card hurried up. He seemed in a terrible rush to show off the Hall.

'Glorious isn't it?!' he said, opening the great doors into the central hallway. 'I always think of it like a dear old uncle who's in need of a little smartening up.'

Tuning out the agent's prattle, Marney drifted through into the house. From the moment he stepped inside he felt reborn. The same sensation had overwhelmed him when Sri Omo-ji had announced the Eighteenth Incarnation. Unable to control himself, he wept.

The estate agent offered the Canadian a silk pocket square on which to dab his eyes.

'How many rooms are there?' Marney asked a little later, once they'd taken in the six reception halls, the grand staircase, and the sunken baths.

'Hard to say, really,' the agent replied. 'Counting the upper floors, it must be nearing the hundred mark.'

'And how much land?'

'Five hundred and fifty-two acres – including two farms, forests, fields, and a model village.'

Marney swallowed hard.

'Is there a back way out – another driveway?'

'Yes, sir. It follows the line of the river.' The agent pinched the end of his chin in thought. 'Not that it would be of interest to a gentleman such as yourself,' he said, 'but there's an extensive network of tunnels running under the entire property and out as far as Stourpaine. They were supposedly built by the first duke – not quite sure why. Once heard something about a pair of mistresses.'

Marney pointed to an especially tall set of walnut doors at the far end of the central hallway.

'What's through there?'

'Thought you'd never ask,' the agent said brightly. 'It's the hexagonal meeting room.'

Even before the doors were opened, Marney pulled out his phone, and sent a text message to the godman's headquarters in Varanasi – MANANA GREEN IS GO! Then, nodding, he sniffed.

'We'll buy it,' he said.

His back warming with delight, the agent calculated his commission.

'Not sure if I made clear, the house and grounds are available in entirety,' he squirmed. 'Or divided into fifteen individual lots.'

Marney frowned, as though the man was an imbecile.

'We'll take it all,' he said.

8

AT THE NEXT evening audience, His Celestial Highness spoke of human failings, highlighting the way those claiming to be honourable or loyal rarely were.

'Life tests us all,' he said. 'It tests us in the opportunities it provides, and in the way it expects us to help those we cherish. But there is no test quite as profound as the test of divine love.'

The *punyas* listened with rapt attention, even those with bandaged heads. Although silent, most of them were desperately hoping Sri Omo-ji would call upon them, putting their love for him to the test.

Behind the auditorium, sitting alone in the office, Bitu watched the projection. All twenty of the hall's cameras were live on the bank of screens – those filming the audience, and others trained on the godman.

Clicking a button on the computer's keyboard, the faces of all eight thousand devotees were framed in miniature digital boxes. A click of the mouse, and the faces changed colour. Depending on a disciple's stress level, they appeared a different shade, from pale blue right through to jet-black.

Sri Omo-ji asked his followers which would die for him.

Every single one put up a hand.

In the office, Bitu noted the faces that stayed pale blue, indicating a stress-free and therefore a loyal state of mind. The software's Israeli developers claimed anyone whose face remained light blue on three key questions was in a different league from the rest.

Thanking the *punyas*, Sri Omo-ji posed a second question:

'Who here would sacrifice their children for the sake

of the Eighteenth Incarnation?'

The query was met with a wave of hushed whispers.

Three-quarters of the devotees put up a hand. As before, Bitu observed which faces stayed light blue.

Grooming a hand down through his beard, the godman addressed the audience a third time:

'Which *poonya* would kill me if I asked them to do so out of divine love?'

Only ten of the followers put up a hand.

Several broke down uncontrollably. Many more begged for forgiveness. But the number of hands to be counted wasn't important. What mattered was how many faces were light blue at the end of all three questions.

Squinting at the projection, Bitu counted.

Nine faces – three men and six women.

9

WHILE WAITING FOR the sale to go through, Marney installed himself at the Crown Hotel four miles south of Pimperne Hall.

Located at the edge of the quiet market town of Blandford Forum, it was opposite the solicitors which the estate agent had recommended. A small country branch of a long-established London firm, Messrs Penshaw, Willis, Smink & Co. was well regarded in the local area for their efficiency and tradition.

Even before sending over photographs of the property or relevant details, Marney had received a reply: 'MAMANA IMMEDIATE', signifying the need to move forward in haste.

As the Canadian crossed West Street for his appointment, he noticed the solicitor's office was located next door to the town's Masonic Lodge. He groaned to himself. There was nothing Marney disapproved of more than secret societies.

Knocking hard, he was buzzed into a cramped office.

The walls were arranged with ancient ledgers, the desk stacked with piles of forgotten paperwork. Curled up on the floor was a Jack Russell. It was missing a back foot, and was wearing a home-made coat.

Basil Wortherly sat up in his chair so as to get a clear view over the files. He couldn't remember the last time a foreigner had ever crossed the threshold. The colour of blinding white paper, the solicitor's skin had rarely if ever been exposed to direct sunlight.

'I am planning to buy Pimperne Hall,' Marney said once introductions and talk of the weather were over.

Moving with slothful slowness, Wortherly picked up a fountain pen and unscrewed the top.

'What is your address?' he asked.

'I have been living in India, and am currently staying at The Crown. I'm buying the house and all its property in the name of my company – Mamana Holdings.'

The details were written down on a legal pad.

'I assume you shall wish to have a full survey done,' the solicitor said.

'That won't be necessary,' Marney responded. 'I want to move in as soon as possible.'

'When did you have in mind, sir?'

'Well, I can get the funds paid through tomorrow, with a view to taking possession at the end of next week.'

10

THE THREE MEN and six women whose faces had remained light blue were put through a series of additional loyalty tests.

These were executed in such a way that the *punyas* involved had no idea they were being tested at all. Every one of them passed with flying colours, confirming their reliability, and that of the expensive Israeli software.

Known as the 'blue faces', the nine-strong team of ultra-loyal devotees were called into a special meeting room which had been swept for listening devices ten minutes earlier. The Maharaja of Patiala briefed them. Having sworn them to secrecy, he gave them numbers – from Blue One to Blue Nine. After that he explained how the ashram was to be abandoned.

'In this new and dangerous time,' he concluded, 'His Highness Sri Omo-ji is calling upon you all to guard him with your lives.'

Once the blue faces had been briefed, the inner circle was told of 'OPERATION VAMOOSE' – the decision to leave Varanasi. As with the blue faces, they were sworn to total secrecy, and ordered not to discuss the plans anywhere within the compound.

The Indian Political Intelligence Office had been sending operatives to the ashram for weeks. Posing as would-be devotees, the spies managed to plant dozens of eavesdropping devices. One-by-one they were winkled out by the Cray Supercomputer, which performed regular background checks on every *poonya*.

As soon as a spy had been identified, they were isolated from the general population. Once extra background checks were completed, they were stripped down to their underwear. With drums beating, and the *punyas* clapping, they were tarred, feathered, and expelled from the compound.

Over a period of ten days, the inner circle worked overtime, getting equipment packed up and smuggled out through the secret tunnel from the pantry.

Zap, the fixer, laid on a fleet of trucks to ferry material assets to Kolkata Port, where they were loaded into specially reinforced sea containers.

Each night groups of devotees were woken and provided with regular street clothes to wear. Allowed ten minutes to pack a single bag, they were blindfolded, and taken to the secret escape tunnel. At the other end buses were standing by to convey the disciples to airports all over India.

Ten days into OPERATION VAMOOSE, the nine blue faces were roused an hour before dawn, and were given street clothes to wear. His expression grave, the Maharaja of Patiala led them down to the secret base deep beneath the ashram, which none of them knew existed.

Sixty-one Louis Vuitton suitcases were lined up, each one stuffed with gifts presented to His Celestial Highness by his adoring *punyas*. An entire case was devoted to jewellery and high-end wristwatches. Another was packed with Versace bedroom slippers. Six more were crammed to bursting with bundles of hundred-dollar notes.

In another section of the Pantry, the Cray Supercomputer had been backed up to a secure online cloud. The hard drives were then removed and physically destroyed. In the central armoury, the weapons were dismantled and loaded into transportation crates.

The atmosphere in the secret underground unit was tense, as though something of monumental importance was taking place. None of the blue faces had ever seen this side of the faith they held in such unquestioning esteem.

Behind a recently installed blast door, the two old friends were sitting alone in the godman's private quarters.

'How the hell did we do it?' Bitu asked in disbelief.

'Do what?'

'All this?!'

'Dunno… just sort of happened. We didn't do it… it did itself.'

Bitu sighed.

'Remember trying to scrape together a few measly rupees back at the Kumbh Mela? Next thing we know there's all this.'

'And thank God for it.'

Bitu did a double take.

'Why d'you say that?'

'Think about it,' Harry said. 'We've given thousands of lost people a direction. We've given them hope, and love… and a sense of community greater than anything they've ever known.'

A buzzer sounded.

Bitu strode over to the blast door, unlocked it, and eased it back with all his strength. Rosco was standing in the frame.

'They're ready for His Celestial Highness,' he said gravely.

Five minutes later, Sri Omo-ji slipped out into the tunnel, the Maharaja of Patiala behind him – both dressed in normal street clothes like everyone else.

Zap had surpassed himself, sourcing long-life heat pads with which to trick the secret service's thermal imaging cameras. Along with looped recorded chanting, cut-outs, and mannequins, they gave the impression that all was normal inside the ashram.

Even more impressive was the fact that he'd managed to get a replacement British passport issued in the name of Hardeep Singh.

11

NEXT DAY, AFTER driving north for many hours in a nondescript coach, His Celestial Highness, Bitu, Zap, the inner circle, and the nine blue faces crossed the border into Nepal.

At Kathmandu's Tribuvan Airport, a chartered Boeing 717 was awaiting them. Once the godman's luggage was stowed safely in the hold, the passengers boarded. Refuelling in Helsinki, the plane landed at Southampton.

Although in street clothes, Omo-ji remained in character.

On the flight he pretended to slip into a prolonged meditation, and resisted the urge to chitchat with Bitu, as they did when they were in private.

Through all the months Harry had posed as Sri Omo-ji, no one had dared to ask where he was from, or what his birth name really was. Most of the devotees assumed he was Indian, but that he'd travelled widely throughout the world. Some of them even believed the elaborate cover story that Two-See's team had built on Wikipedia and elsewhere... a tall tale involving divine revelations and sacred water at a hermitage in the Himalayas.

At Southampton Airport's immigration counter, the godman whispered to Bitu to send the blue faces through. Not wishing to leave their guru, they resisted at first.

Once alone, Harry slipped his British passport onto

the scanner and was admitted back into the United Kingdom. A few feet away, Bitu presented the officer with a brand-new Slovakian passport bearing his photograph and the name Vladimír Kotleba.

Like everything else, it was sourced by the fixer who'd long since proved he could fix the unfixable, and who was next in line, also travelling as a Slovak.

Bitu's document was checked under an ultraviolet light, then with a loupe, and Vladimír Kotleba entered England for the first time.

Standing away from the baggage reclaim, Harry winked to his friend. Surrounded by the nine blue faces, he didn't dare lower his guard. Feigning an air of apathy, he masked the jubilation at being home. Out by the kerb an emerald-green Maybach was waiting.

As soon as Harry was safely inside, Blue Face One climbed in the front. Sri Omo-ji's luggage was loaded into a series of Mercedes vans, the inner circle and remaining blue faces climbing into half a dozen more.

An hour after landing, the godman and his entourage were driving through the peaceful winding country roads of the Dorset countryside. Sitting beside Bitu, Harry reached out and slapped his friend on the knee.

'Can't believe we're home!' he said.

12

FIVE MINUTES FROM Pimperne Hall, the convoy paused at the White Horse pub so His Celestial Highness could change into his robes.

Rosco begged that a more suitable place be found to stop, but Sri Omo-ji insisted. Carrying in the godman's Louis Vuitton suitcase, the Maharaja of Patiala requested that everyone else remain in the vehicles.

As soon as he and the guru were inside, Bitu made a beeline for the toilets.

'What's the rush?!' Harry called.

Turning, Bitu saw the godman ambling up to the bar.

'Two pints of bitter, please,' he said.

Taking him for any other punter, the publican pulled two glasses of the local Badger Ale. Harry and Bitu clinked, wiped the foam from their lips, and thanked their good fortune.

'Got something for you,' Harry said.

'What?'

'A gift.'

Bitu looked at his friend mistrustfully.

'Why?'

'Because you're the best of the best.'

Reaching into his Louis Vuitton case, he removed a parcel wrapped in plush silver paper.

'Go on, have a look.'

Even more mistrustful than before, Bitu tore away the paper.

Inside was an exquisite mahogany box. Pulling back the lid, he set eyes on a wristwatch.

Harry leaned in.

'It's a Patek Philippe Grandmaster Chime in rose gold,' he said. 'Rarest of the rare.'

His friend's lower jaw dropped.

'This was in the news,' he said. 'Most expensive watch in the world. Sold at auction for…'

'*Thirty-three million dollars*,' Harry whispered.

Bitu blinked thanks.

As he did so he caught a flash of himself trudging down Blackpool pier in the rain, a polystyrene cup of milky tea in each hand.

'Time to get changed,' Harry said, downing his bitter.

Five minutes after that, His Celestial Highness Sri Omo-ji sashayed through, now dressed in a voluminous turban and emerald-green robes, his neck festooned in gold chains and an assortment of necklaces. Similarly attired in the livery of the Eighteenth Incarnation, the Maharaja of Patiala trailed close behind.

As the door to the toilets swung open the publican glanced up and grinned.

'Fancy dress party tonight is there, boys?!' he cried.

13

THE MAYBACH CRUISED through the crested gates of Pimperne Hall, and crawled along the three-mile driveway at walking pace, allowing His Celestial Highness to take in the landscape.

On the back seat, Bitu grunted.

'You ready?'

Harry flicked his head down in a nod.

Taking the last bend, the limousine halted a short distance from Pimperne Hall. Between the car and the house was an eight-thousand-strong crowd of devotees. All wearing identical emerald-green robes, they knelt in unison, hands over their faces in honour of Sri Omo-ji.

'Jesus Christ,' Bitu groaned under his breath. 'Marney's outdone himself.'

'Not bad,' the godman added with understatement. 'Looks like everyone got here.'

The Maybach's door was opened by the driver liveried in green, and the godman stepped onto a green carpet.

As he glided forwards to the house, hands pressed together in *Namaste*, an army of children hurried up, scattering green rose petals at his feet.

Kneeling at the front of the house, Marney hoped the guru would single him out for praise.

But he did not.

Instead, Sri Omo-ji walked past, his emerald-green Versace slippers padding silently into the house.

14

THE FIRST TWO months of life at Pimperne Hall were marked with fervent activity, the *punyas* working shifts round the clock.

Zap the fixer spread rumours in the local area that

a charity music festival, called 'Greenstock', was taking place. It explained why so many thousands of people dressed in varying shades of green were descending on the quiet corner of Dorset.

While still under the radar of the British establishment, the devotees embarked on a raft of ambitious plans. The first job undertaken was to upgrade Pimperne Hall, especially the areas reserved for His Celestial Highness. The private living quarters were fitted out with luxury furnishings, and with the latest security gear.

As at the ashram in Varanasi, a secret lift descended to a bunker – one that none of the rank-and-file *punyas* knew existed. Fully autonomous from the main house, it housed the usual range of facilities – including a communication hub, an armoury, a gym, a cinema, as well as walk-in bank vaults, storerooms, and escape systems.

Outside the house, the devotees set about constructing a hexagonal auditorium the size of a soccer pitch, called the 'Great Hall of Verdant Sanctity'. Once it was completed, they built a hospital, two schools, and a multitude of office buildings. So as not to contravene the area's strict planning laws, many of the new buildings were recessed into the ground. As an afterthought, Pimperne Hall's farm buildings were modernized, the fields ploughed, and sown with crops.

With donations pouring in from all over the world, there was no shortage of funds for even the most extravagant plans. Rosco, who was in charge of investments, made millions more through his connections in Silicon Valley.

Meanwhile, a nature trail was laid out in the forest along the banks of the River Stour. For the first time in the property's history, the habitat was protected from huntsmen.

A bookstore, cinema, beauty salon, and bowling alley were constructed, too, as well as a boutique packed with clothing – all of it in vibrant emerald green.

Another shop on the compound, The Sri Omo-ji Emporium, stocked hundreds of products relating to the godman. Everything on offer bore the guru's face – from tear-off calendars, dishcloths embroidered with proverbs, board games, and of course the bestseller, *The Path of Omo*.

Most important of all, an enormous rock was delivered on a flat-loader, the kind designed to transport military tanks. Embossed with the odd hexagonal symbol, it was even more impressive than the original Great Stone, abandoned at the ashram in Varanasi.

15

MR AND MRS Singh were slumped on the sofa in the front room at 10 Henry Street, as they were every evening between the hours of six and ten.

The ritual was always the same:

Four hours of game shows, reality TV, and the odd

Hindi classic thrown in, with supper served on their laps. Ranjit Singh would make sure the kitchen was always stocked with plenty of off-cuts. Some of the meat may have been well past its sell-by date, but his wife piled on the spices so much that they never noticed. A lifetime in butchery had blessed them both with cast-iron stomachs.

At six o'clock, Mr Singh burped long and hard, then reached for the remote control.

'What about an oldie?' he grunted. 'I'm in the mood for *36 Chowringhee Lane*.'

'You and your Shashi Kapoor, Ranjit!'

'Quiet, you like him as much as me.'

Burping again, Mr Singh turned on the TV and began making the long journey to Amazon Prime. Technically challenged to the point of absurdity, the Singhs spent almost as much time each night finding the right show as they did watching it. The process involved flicking their way through hundreds of channels one-by-one.

While Ranjit Singh hunted, his wife put on her bifocals.

'Keeps taking me to that damned Sky News,' he growled. 'Nothing I hate more than Sky!'

'Shall I do it? I've got my glasses on.'

'Hush! I will find it! You're no good with this thing!'

In the world of Mr Singh, the TV remote was a weapon never to be relinquished from the grasp of a man. His thumb aching, he rested for a moment.

Inexplicably, Sky News flashed up again.

'I'll just catch the headlines,' he said firmly.

'Thought you hated Sky.'

'I do! But a man must see the news to know what's going on.'

Turning to face the other camera for the next item, the anchor read her script:

'And now for something that strains the boundaries of plausibility… An Indian guru who's set up an ashram in a sleepy Dorset village is enraging locals with a world of free love and miracles, all of it washed in emerald green. We managed to get a secret camera inside. Hugh Thomas has the story.'

A well-presented Englishman explained how he was donning sacred robes and a secret body-cam to lift the lid on the Path of Omo. After a quick piece-to-camera he was shown emerging in the grounds of Pimperne Hall, his voice stressed to breaking point.

'I'm now in the ashram of His Celestial Highness Sri Omo-ji,' he whispered, 'whose Eighteenth Incarnation is taking place not in the wilds of far-away India from where he's come, but at a leafy West Country retreat. The cult's devotees are all heading into the Great Hall of Verdant Sanctity, where the guru is about address them.'

A series of indistinct shots followed, while the secret camera struggled to focus. Then, amid a tremendous swishing noise, the undercover reporter managed to pan over a sea of people in emerald green. There were thousands upon thousands of them. Many missing ears and a few missing their thumbs.

Their curiosity piqued, the Singhs watched.

'Bloody nonsense!' Mr Singh barked.

'Look at them all,' his wife muttered.

'It's a shame on India. No wonder everyone gives us so much trouble.'

Slowly, the camera focused on a lone heavily bearded figure seated on the stage.

Mrs Singh nudged the bifocals up her nose.

'Wait a minute, Ranjit...' she said.

'Wait a minute, *what*?'

'That guru... look at him.'

'What about him?'

Mrs Singh gasped.

'He looks like Hardeep!'

Her husband grunted.

'Well it's not. That crook sitting there has fame and fortune – two things lazy good-for-nothing Hardeep will never have!'

'But I'm sure it's him!'

His face flushed, Mr Singh grabbed the remote control and turned the TV off.

'I've told you a hundred times, never to mention his name in this house!' he cried.

16

AT THE FAR end of the gardens stood an ancient oak,

its colossal trunk etched with the initials of lovers stretching back a century and more, the boughs alive with birdsong.

As the shadows lengthened each day, afternoon ebbing towards dusk, Karnika would sit alone beneath the oak and pray for the soul of Sri Omo-ji.

From the other end of the gardens Marney would watch her sitting there in the lotus position, a vision of feminine beauty. Shy by nature, he couldn't quite bring himself to go over and sit with her.

But then one morning Karnika made eye contact with the timid Canadian in the breakfast queue, and she smiled. Not the absent smile of one acquaintance to another, but a smile of enduring affection.

That evening, Marney waited for Karnika to take up her position. As soon as he spied her there, he made a beeline to where she was sitting beneath the oak.

Her eyes firmly closed, back ramrod straight, she smiled as the Canadian approached.

'Been hoping you'd join me here,' she said with a grin.

Marney was overcome with lust.

'How d'you know who it is?' he asked gingerly.

'X-ray vision,' Karnika replied with a laugh. 'Come sit down beside me. Come close.'

Marney did as he was told, and there began a love affair the likes of which he'd never known. Love for a woman who understood him, and loved him in return.

Over the following days, the pair became inseparably

close. They shared every detail of one another's lives. Confiding secrets and exchanging whims, they laughed and wept together. Most profound of all was that their love for Sri Omo-ji was mirrored in the other, as though viewed in the sacred lens of a kaleidoscope.

One evening as they sat close together beneath the oak, Karnika stroked a hand over Marney's knee.

'I loved you from the first moment I saw you,' she said tenderly.

'And I loved you even before that,' the Canadian replied.

Leaning in, they touched lips in a kiss.

Hush prevailed, until the last strains of light gave in to darkness. Never in his life had Marney been so close to anyone that he was comfortable in their silence. He was about to pledge his eternal love, but Karnika spoke first.

'You know I share my love for you,' she said.

'And I mine for you.'

'To think He's so selfless that He's asked us all not to love Him... not to worship Him.'

Marney's eyes welled with tears.

'It's the only request of His I can't agree to.'

Karnika sighed.

'I feel as though my soul is knitted up to His.'

'I'd die for Him.'

'So would I... and even then the sacrifice would be

too little.'

Leaning in, they kissed again.

As they did so, Karnika shivered.

'You OK darling?'

'Yeah. Just got spooked, I suppose.'

'D'you see something out there?'

'No, no, it was something I thought of.'

Marney wrapped his arms around her, and held her tight.

'Don't be frightened, I'm here.'

'I had a terrible dream last night,' Karnika whispered. 'I dreamed that Sri Omo-ji went to sleep and didn't wake up.'

'Don't say such things!'

'But what if it happened?'

Almost choking at the thought, Marney smoothed a hand down Karnika's hair.

'Our lives are in His hands,' he answered, 'and we are here to serve Him, to protect Him.'

Again, Karnika shivered.

'Perhaps,' she uttered in a voice so quiet as to be almost silent, 'perhaps it would be better for Sri Omo-ji not to live.'

Unsure he'd heard the comment correctly, Marney pulled back, his bloodstream becoming fortified with adrenalin.

'What d'you say?!' he voiced with alarm.

'It's just that things are so perfect, so serene. I'm

worried they'll go off the rails.'

Reeling, Marney was at a loss for words.

'He MUST live,' he responded resolutely. 'And nothing – and I mean *nothing* – is gonna go off the rails!'

Karnika shuddered a third time, more forcefully than before.

'I hope and pray things stay as they are for an eternity,' she said.

17

OVER THE FIRST hundred days Sri Omo-ji made the occasional appearance in the great hall, but remained largely hidden from view.

While the inner circle spread word he was praying for the souls of the Unloved Children, a rumour circulated that he was unwell – still weakened by the long hibernation.

The truth was rather different.

Having escaped from Pimperne Hall through the tunnels, Harry and Bitu had taken a taxi to Salisbury, then the train up to London and on to Blackpool. Dressed in regular clothes, they successfully cultivated a high-end hipster look.

At Salisbury railway station, Bitu took out a wad of crisp fifty-pound notes and asked for two first class return tickets.

Harry nudged him hard.

'Let's go second class.'

'Whatever for?'

'For a taste of how things used to be.'

Late in the afternoon the train rolled into Blackpool North Station.

'First stop where it all began,' Harry said.

'Where's that?'

'Where The Great Maharaja Malipasse dropped dead.'

Strolling the half-mile stretch down Talbot Road, they reached the North Pier at sunset. Minds clouded with memories, Harry and Bitu ambled down the pier, pausing at the spot where on that soaking day they'd walked out on their old lives.

'Back then we were nobodies,' Bitu said reflectively.

'No we weren't,' Harry shot back. 'We were who we are now, but no one else knew it.'

'Wish I'd have known it would end as well as it has.'

'If you'd have known it the journey would've been impossible,' Harry said. 'We had to jump through the hoops to be exactly where we are.'

That evening at a hole-in-the-wall diner across from the football stadium they devoured a feast of black pudding, mushy peas, and fish and chips, washed down with Boddingtons bitter. The walls were layered in a film of beige grease, accumulated through decades of serving up what Marlene, the owner, called 'Heart Attack on a Plate'. An officious old battle-axe, she took the orders at the counter. Bent double much of the time by a smoker's cough, she was as much an institution as the diner itself.

'Beats our friggin' chef and the posh dinner plates,' Harry said, a hand clasped to his stomach.

'Maybe we could get a place like this done at Pimperne,' Bitu suggested. 'I'm sure Marlene would be willing to branch out.'

'Can't believe she hasn't recognized us,' Harry grumbled. 'I've been coming in here since I was a kid.'

'C'mon,' Bitu answered, 'let's get to bed.'

Vetoing Travelodge as being too up-market, Harry had insisted they stay at a low-end B&B on Henry Street. Deficient in every way, it was two doors down from the Singh family home. They took the most modest rooms with a shared bathroom.

At breakfast next morning both asked for the 'full English'.

Blustering back to the kitchen, a trail of cigarette smoke following her, the landlady got the frying pan out.

'Mrs Jeffries doesn't recognize me either!' Harry snapped. 'Jesus Christ! I've known her forever. Her bloody son Marty used to duff me up every break time.'

Bitu opened the morning's copy of *The Sun* which was perched at the edge of the table.

'It's not the same since they got rid of Page Three,' he muttered. 'There's nothing else worth looking at in here.'

Mrs Jeffries lurched through the door, a plate of fried fare in either hand.

'Hope you two like ya eggs well done, boys,' she said. 'I do them how my son Martin likes them. Course he can do them a whole lot better than me. He's a chef in Manchester. Got his own restaurant, he has.'

Harry was about to shoot out a suitable reply, when his gaze fell on the red-top's front page. A massive headline blared:

INVASION OF
THE GREEN GURU!

Leaping up, Harry told Bitu to pay the bill, while he messaged Zap to lay on emergency transport back to Dorset.

As he stood on Henry Street, his mother and father came out of their house and walked straight past him.

They were arguing in Punjabi about the best way to cook spinach.

18

A MAN WHO loathed confrontation, Marney found reasons to avoid his beloved Karnika rather than try and make sense of her inexplicable comment.

Uneasy in one another's company, they each made excuses as to why they couldn't spend time together.

The divide deepened.

Within a week their love affair was dead.

Karnika stopped meditating beneath the oak, and spent her time sitting on the bench beside the Great Stone. But rather than meditating, she was seen mumbling to herself. With every day that passed, her hair and clothing appeared a little more unkempt, as though she were suffering from some kind of malady.

Keeping a distance, Marney monitored Karnika, worrying and wondering if he ought to speak out to other members of the inner circle. Each time he had made up his mind to break his silence, something caused him to hold back.

Unable to keep the secret of Karnika's deranged state any longer, he was about to send a message to the members of the inner circle, expressing an urgent need to speak to them, when the Maharaja of Patiala called an extraordinary assembly. All members of the inner circle and the blue faces were requested to make their way immediately to the hexagonal meeting room. Filing in with the others, Marney scanned the room for Karnika.

She wasn't there.

The rushed return from Blackpool had involved a chartered Sikorsky S92 helicopter scooping Harry and Bitu up from Stanley Park, and depositing them in a field outside Pimperne.

Slipping down into the labyrinth of tunnels, they found the fixer waiting for them with a golf cart. Before they knew it, they were in the godman's private apartments.

Ten minutes later, they were in costume and in character at an emergency meeting.

The Maharaja of Patiala addressed the trusted devotees on the godman's behalf, while His Celestial

Highness sat in silence.

'It was just a matter of time before the press heard about us,' he said, holding up the crumpled copy of the morning's *Sun*.

'Journalists have been snooping around for the last week or two,' Marney reported.

'Bet they were tipped off by the guy at the Anvil Inn,' Rosco said darkly. 'He's had it in for us since Day One.'

The Maharaja cracked his knuckles.

'We've got to lock down,' he said. 'That means barbed wire and laser alarms until we get a ten-foot wall built around the entire property. We need to ramp up security on the gates, and put thermal cameras in the grounds. From now on, everyone coming in or out gets screened.'

Stepping forwards, Marney put up a hand.

'I think we ought to check everyone already within the perimeter,' he said loudly. 'And I mean *everyone*!'

The Maharaja shot the Canadian an unspoken instruction to sit down. As soon as Marney was seated, Rosco leapt to his feet.

'Your Highness, the problem is the locals in Pimperne and Stourpaine,' he blurted. 'They don't trust anyone wearing green, and are calling us a "cult".'

Motionless, Sri Omo-ji cleared his throat softly, indicating for the Maharaja to approach him. When Bitu's ear was in line with his mouth, the godman's lips parted and he whispered something.

Striding back to the trusted inner circle, the Maharaja

cracked his knuckles again.

'His Celestial Highness says we are to buy the villages,' he said.

'Which one?' asked Rosco.

'Pimperne and Stourpaine... and all the surrounding farmland as well.'

19

THE REPORTS ON Sky News and in *The Sun* were only the beginning.

Within a week of the story breaking, a full press corps was camped out at the ashram's gates. Every reporter had the same question –

Who is the mysterious Indian godman, and why has he chosen such a secluded corner of rural Dorset?

The devotees took it in turns to patrol the grounds while the barbed wire fencing was put in place. At the same time, the ashram set up a press office, and invited select journalists in to tour the campus on what was the first major charm offensive.

Given the role of chief publicity officer, Karnika conducted the tours. From the start it was made clear the reporters would not be permitted to speak to His Celestial Highness, nor would they be free to roam anywhere they wished. When asked why, they were told it was out of a need to maintain DSHW – Divine Silence of the Higher Way.

Having been dispatched to cover the community's

rise, the droves of journalists were on a mission to advance the story. After all, a worldwide audience was intrigued by the bizarre antics of the green-cloaked godman. In the name of sales, the best investigative journalists in the business dropped everything and drilled down into the underbelly of Sri Omo-ji's life.

Fleet Street's finest ran a stream of stories, describing drug-crazed pandemonium at Pimperne Hall. At the same time, the fixer extraordinaire countered it with a wall of misinformation worthy of any secret service.

With the help of Two-See, he planted a treasure trail of articles online for the press to ferret out. They included a detailed history of the guru's childhood in rural Punjab, and dozens of first-person accounts of his charity and selflessness.

But the most effective campaign was the one bankrolled by Rosco P Schultz III. Digging into his savings, he hired Hollywood's leading agents to serve up a glittering array of A-listers. Paid a million dollars each, they made a beeline to Pimperne Hall, ready to sing their support for the enlightened Way of Sri Omo-ji.

20

IN ALL, A hundred stars were choppered in, to celebrate one hundred days since His Celestial Highness's arrival in England.

Among them were the great and the good of Hollywood, with country and western music legends, folk singers, rappers, and two boy bands.

Amid razzmatazz worthy of a rock concert, the visiting celebrities, the inner circle, the blue faces, and thousands of rank-and-file *punyas* filed into the Great Hall of Verdant Sanctity.

All visitors were requested to dress in emerald-green robes irrespective of who they were. The only exception made was to one of the more eccentric A-listers, who had turned up with a pair of pet albino leopards straining on solid gold chains. At being invited to don the requisite emerald-green robes, he had a tantrum and was bustled inside.

With the devotees sitting cross-legged in silence on the floor of the hexagonal hall, the house lights dimmed.

'Believe' by Cher was played loud through speakers hidden in the floor, the air scented with crushed lemongrass. The hundred celebrities climbed onto the stage, and performed a ballad written only hours before. In praise of the godman, it was called 'Prelude to Mystery'.

As the ballad ended, the A-listers took their places among the devotees. Then, the Bulgarians began drumming the timpani slow and hard, as they'd done through the weeks of human hibernation.

His Celestial Highness wafted onto the stage through the emerald-green curtains.

Setting eyes on their leader, the *punyas* broke into spontaneous applause – covering their faces with their hands, as they yelled: '*Mamana!*'

Sri Omo-ji greeted his followers and the distinguished guests, then signalled for silence. Stepping over to a furry white armchair, he paused to collect his thoughts. The gaze of the audience on him, and the video cameras streaming the images to millions of people all over the world, Sri Omo-ji laughed.

Not the kind of laughter that follows in the wake of a joke, but laughter of a completely different kind. Playful and yet discordant, it was the kind of laughter everyone has inside them but never dares to release.

The laughter ended as instantaneously as it had begun, and the godman tapped the tip of a finger to the microphone.

'Humans fear what they don't understand,' he said. 'And at the same time they cling hold of what they do understand, even if it's wrong. Like someone shipwrecked, they are adrift. Instead of freeing themselves from the driftwood, they hold it so tight that it prevents them from taking hold of something else – something which might actually save them.'

Pausing to take breath, Sri Omo-ji stood up. Gliding over to a microphone on a stand at the front of the stage, he gazed down at the devotees.

'People say I'm a mind-controller and that this is a cult,' he said. 'To them I reply they're wrong on both counts. I am not *me*, but *we*. And *you* are not you, but *me*. We are part of one another, united in a belief in honesty and in our love for the truth.' His voice faltering, the guru touched a hand to his heart. 'I am sick of secrets,' he said. 'The secrets that suffocate us, and eat into our lives. What if we could be free of them – free of all the secrets? I cannot tell you what to do, but I can set an example. So, if you will allow me, I will tell you a secret that hangs over me like a sword dangling on a thread…'

The godman was about to deliver the next line when Karnika leapt to her feet and vaulted up onto the stage.

Her fist was clenched around the shaft of a long carving knife.

Time seemed to stop, then advance one frame at a time.

The audience inhaled in horror, and exhaled in screams.

Speeding forward, Karnika lunged.

Sri Omo-ji twisted sideways.

Again, Karnika lunged, harder than before, her face a mask of rage.

The *punyas* were propelled into hysteria.

The blade sliced into the godman's shoulder.

Pulling it back, Karnika struck a second time, as the godman's roar of pain was drowned out by the audience.

21

A TV AUDIENCE of millions watched as the nine blue faces leapt out from the wings, and wrestled the would-be assassin to the ground. Shielding Sri Omo-ji with their bodies, they hurried him away.

Down below, the devotees jumped up in horror, screaming, remonstrating, hugging, howling as though they themselves had been attacked. As they did so, Karnika was knocked unconscious, and dragged outside.

The VIP guests and the albino leopards were ushered away to a safe room by the inner circle, who feared another assault. Amid a scene of pandemonium, the few TV crews who'd been invited wasted no time in doing live pieces to camera.

Strapped to a stretcher, the guru was rushed to the hospital building, in the shadow of Pimperne Hall. While he was sped through into the operating theatre, ten units of his blood were retrieved from his personal blood-bank. A three-hour operation followed, at the end of which the surgeon pronounced the procedure a success.

Even before the guru had been prepared for surgery, Karnika was being roused with smelling salts and cuffed.

As the former love of his life was whisked away to the local police station in Blandford, Marney fell onto the ground, head between his hands.

'It's all my fault!' he wept. 'I should have told them what I knew!'

After all the excitement, the celebrity A-listers clambered back into the helicopters and were flown away from the ashram. Then, once their news stories had been filed, the press pack was escorted off the premises.

His private apartments guarded by a security team, Sri Omo-ji admitted no visitors except for medical personnel and the Maharaja of Patiala. News of His Celestial Highness's condition was circulated to the *punyas* twice daily, and prayers for his speedy recovery were held in the Great Hall of Verdant Sanctity.

With the assassination attempt being so high profile, the local police at Blandford began making their investigation. The team of officers was joined by a thirty-strong unit sent by Special Branch.

Reporting to MI5, they swept every inch of the ashram. Or rather, they swept what they imagined to be every inch. They missed the godman's second private apartment above ground, as well as the secret bunker and the tunnels.

22

FOR SEVEN DAYS and nights the devotees threw themselves into prayer – beseeching the powers of the universe to protect their beloved guru. The crisis ushered forth a period of manic devotion in what was the most extraordinary phase so far of the Sri Omo-ji faith.

Developing over nights and days, it took the form of clear stages.

The first stage saw every single *poonya* hurry onto the paddock beyond the great oak tree, as though led there by the Pied Piper. Trooping forth, stamping feet and chanting '*Mamana!*' they formed a colossal human chain. Spiralling round and round, and doubling back on itself, the string of believers if seen from above spelled out the name 'OMO'.

A second phase saw the *punyas* falling to their knees and crawling everywhere in an act of atonement. Those who didn't conform were quickly shunned. Within a day and a half there wasn't a single follower at Pimperne Hall on two feet.

The third phase began when a Latvian devotee took a meat cleaver from the kitchens, crawled out to the Great Stone, and hacked off his right thumb. Instead of bandaging the wound, he allowed the stream of blood to flow, anointing his forehead with it.

News of the penance quickly spread.

Within minutes, devotees were scurrying to the Great Stone on hands and knees, and lining up to amputate a thumb as well. By nightfall, three thousand digits had been piled up in a bloodied monument at the front of Pimperne Hall.

Through days and nights the atmosphere of hysteria mounted, as the *punyas* punished themselves for the attempt on their guru's life. Breaking into small groups, some missing ears as well as thumbs, faces stained red, they voiced their fear in whispers.

Despite the regular news bulletins, rumours spread. One was that Sri Omo-ji was in a coma. Another suggested the only way he stood a chance of pulling through was if more blood was spilled in his name.

A fresh act of penance followed in which the devotees gashed themselves, filling up mugs, bottles, and anything they could find, with blood.

Racing forwards on all fours they took their offerings to the Great Stone, where a transparent tank was quickly filled. As the donations coagulated, and quickly began to stink, a group of Scandinavian followers stripped naked. Rubbing themselves all over with the congealed blood, they crawled away to the shade of the great oak.

23

THE ONLY CORNER not affected by the acts of penance was the room in which Sri Omo-ji was recovering.

Ten days after the attempt on his life, the guru was sitting up in bed, surrounded with cards and flowers – all of them green. The door opened a crack and Bitu swanned in carrying *Time* magazine.

'You made the cover!' he beamed, holding up the latest issue.

Harry read out the headline:

'*Omo-ji: Angel or Demon?*'

'An excellent photo,' Bitu said.

'What d'you mean? It's awful. I hardly recognize myself with this bloody beard.'

'The *punyas*, they've all gone crazy.'

'You mean they've gone "crazier"?'

Glancing at the door, Bitu squirmed.

'It's impossible to describe what's going on. Never seen anything like it.' His mood brightening, he added: 'You should bloody get stabbed more often – it's been amazing for business. Twenty-five million hits on the website, and of those, twenty-three million have signed up. People are turning up day and night from all corners of the Earth.'

'More potential assassins coming to rub out good old Omo-ji?' Harry responded grimly.

'New *punyas* only get admitted once they've passed a full background check,' said Bitu pointedly. 'We've got a whole department crunching the profiles. To think that we trusted Karnika.'

'Why the hell did she do it?!' Harry asked.

'She told the police she was frightened you'd give in to the money and the fame.'

Harry balked at the remark.

'Damn her! Thought she liked me. Thought they all liked me!'

'She does, and they do! They all *love* you!'

'Well stabbing someone in the shoulder with a carving knife isn't my idea of love.'

Bitu groaned.

'Bloody twisted madness, that's what it is!' he said. 'Karnika loves you so much she wanted you to stay perfect and pure.'

Harry scowled.

'Isn't that why the guy shot John Lennon?'

'Dunno.'

'What's happened to her?'

'After she's served her sentence for attempted murder they'll deport her.'

Harry reached out and grabbed his friend's arm.

'I knew it was going to happen,' he said.

'What the hell d'you mean?'

'A premonition.'

'What?'

'Had it five minutes before going on stage. Saw every detail. Even knew the make of the knife – a Sabatier… just as I knew her motive.'

'Why didn't you say something?'

'Because it was fate,' Harry whispered. 'The kind of fate you've gotta take between the eyes… or at least below the shoulder.'

'We've stepped up security,' Bitu replied. 'Zap got us a team of South African mercenaries. They'll shadow you.'

'Shadow me *where*?'

'Everywhere.'

Harry rolled his eyes.

'It's bad enough having eight thousand disciples out there in psycho central,' he said. 'But to have assassins stalking me, and a crack team of South Africans stalking them… that's too much, Bitu-bhai.'

'A lot of new people have come. There are fifteen thousand, not eight thousand.'

'Great!' Harry responded sarcastically.

'*It is!*' his friend answered.

'Yeah?'

'Yes!'

'How exactly is it so friggin' marvellous? Tell me that.'

'Because we're bloody loaded – that's why!'

Harry groaned.

'I don't care about the money. Never did. All I wanted was to prove I had what it took to pull off the great illusion… and I think you'll agree I've done that.'

'*So?*'

'What I'm saying is that I want to disappear.'

'Harry! Listen to yourself!'

'I am! I just don't want to go on.'

Clenching his fists, Bitu shook them.

'I wasn't supposed to tell you this but the *punyas* have bought you a present… a kind of get-well-soon gift.'

'What is it?'

'A green Ferrari.'

'Another one?'

'Very nice green, inside and out.'

'That's the last thing I want, let alone need.'

Bitu smacked his hands together gruffly.

'So what do you want?'

Harry didn't reply, not at first. After a minute-long pause he said:

'I want to go back to my old life, mate.'

24

A WEEK LATER, His Celestial Highness took his first stroll in Pimperne Hall's gardens, the South African close protection team shadowing him every inch of the way.

Out in the grounds, the devotees paused from their duties as soon as they spotted Sri Omo-ji. Many were still on all fours, hands and heads bandaged. Prostrating themselves towards him, they wept in joy, and in sorrow that their beloved guru had come so close to death.

Across from the main house, four thousand newly arrived would-be disciples were filling out application forms and waiting until their number was called. In charge of the intakes, Marney was making sure the extensive background checks were done. Working with a team of translators, he gave each applicant an interview and looked through their paperwork. Most of the new arrivals were quizzed on why they wanted to follow His Celestial Highness at all.

Exhausted from processing so many hundreds of applications, Marney asked the next applicant to step forward. Without even focusing on his face, he scanned the man's form. The passport photo attached to it seemed familiar.

Marney looked up.

'Basil Wortherly?' he said.

'Yes, sir.'

'Basil Wortherly, as in Basil Wortherly of...'

'Formerly of Messrs Penshaw, Willis, Smink & Co., sir.'

'Happy to have you here. But can I ask, why did you want to make the change?'

Straightening his back triumphantly, Basil Wortherly punched a fist in the air.

'Because the world needs fewer dull solicitors,' he said, 'and far more Peace and Love!'

25

THE DAY AFTER, Harry and Bitu locked themselves in the secure bunker and spent nine hours together going over every detail of the world they'd created.

They made a plan – not for a week, a month, or even a year – but a plan stretching decades into the future. A comprehensive structure by which the community could run in perpetuity, it was built on core values and sound investments.

They planned for ashrams to be established on every continent, devoted to the Path of Omo – and for the profits to be paid into a central fund. The publishing and wider media enterprises would be developed, dedicated to spreading the word of Peace and Love.

Most importantly, they made a plan for an external committee to be set up unrelated to the followers. Its mission was to select charitable projects all over the world and to fund them anonymously with income provided by the Omo-ji Ashrams.

One morning a few days after the bunker meeting, the godman and Maharaja asked the inner circle and the nine blue faces to gather in the hexagonal assembly room.

Agitated at being summoned, the trusted devotees stood in silence, eyes trained on the floor.

After a short interval, the Maharaja of Patiala entered.

'The attempt on our beloved Sri Omo-ji's life proved calamities can happen,' he said. 'It also proved the need for planning, and for being far more organized than we've been until now. It's my hope His Highness will be here for many years to come. But,' he said, his voice trembling, 'no one can be certain of the future – not even a living god.'

At that moment the godman paced in, a large padded envelope in his hand, his expression as solemn as that of his friend.

'If anything were ever to happen to us,' he said, 'all the information required to continue is contained in this. It will be placed in Safe No. 6. Every instruction must be followed to the letter.'

Sri Omo-ji regarded the inner circle and the blue faces, his expression uncharacteristically austere.

'We have built an extraordinary organization together… an organization for good,' he said. 'Protect it, and it will protect you. Honour it, and it will honour us all.'

26

THE FOLLOWING AFTERNOON, the Maharaja sent for Zap to meet him at a particular bench out in the garden.

Approaching slowly, the fixer leaned down to touch the aristocrat's feet.

'No need for that,' Bitu said with a smile.

'Just keeping up appearances, sir.'

'Sit down beside me.'

With Zap seated, they paused in silence for a long while.

'You're the one man who knows our secret,' Bitu said softly, staring out at a cluster of devotees tending a flowerbed in the distance.

Turning to look at the Maharaja, he wondered whether being the guardian of such information could have put his life in danger.

'I hardly even remember it,' he replied.

'Of course you do. You know as well as Harry and me we're as ordinary as anyone else.'

'You may have been ordinary at one time, sir,' the fixer answered. 'But there's nothing ordinary about you now.'

Bitu's gaze shifted from the gardens, onto Zap's face.

'We want to ask for your help,' he said.

'Of course... anything you wish.'

After another prolonged silence, Bitu said:

'We are ready to leave.'

'Certainly. I'll have one of the planes made ready. Where would you like to...?'

'No, no, no,' Bitu broke in. 'Not leave for a trip. We want to leave for good.'

The fixer blinked incredulously.

'You mean *disappear*?'

'Precisely. We want to vanish.'

Zap cracked his knuckles one at a time.

'That can be arranged.'

'Good.'

'Is there a plan to follow?'

'We'll leave it up to you. I'm sure you can come up with an appropriate accident.'

'If you insist, sir.'

Bitu smiled again.

'We'll call it OPERATION MISHAP.'

'OK.'

'Other than you, no one's to know. Not anyone... d'you understand?'

Zap wobbled his head.

'One last thing,' Bitu said, his gaze sweeping out over the gardens again. 'Harry wants to get rid of everything he's been given.'

'Everything, sir?'

'Yes, *everything*.'

27

TWO WEEKS PASSED, in which Zap quietly disposed of every single gift presented to Sri Omo-ji, and all the valuable assets he owned.

Diamond-encrusted wristwatches, jewellery, sports cars, and a matching pair of Cessna Citation jets – all of them sold, the funds deposited in the ashram's accounts.

By day the fixer used his network of contacts to sell, sell, sell. And, by night he was kept awake by worry. As the only person alive who shared Harry and Bitu's secret, he feared for his safety. He'd considered writing an affidavit, but what was the point? After all, no one at the ashram would have believed him were he ever to speak out.

One night, while Zap lay in bed, his mind racing, Harry was woken by fears of his own. Unable to get back to sleep, he padded through into his friend's suite.

'Bitu-bhai!' he hissed. 'Wake up!'

'*Huh*? What? What is it?'

'It won't work,' Harry said.

'*What*?'

'You heard me.'

Bitu fumbled for the light switch.

'What's got into you?'

'It's not gonna work!'

'Of course it will, Harry! Zap's got it all planned out.'

Bitu groaned.

'OK! I'll tell him to hold off. That way, you'll have time to think it over.'

Harry let out a long sigh.

'Thank you, *bhaia*.'

Bitu sent a text message to Zap.

It read: ABORT OPERATION MISHAP!

Instantly, a reply came in: FULLY UNDERSTOOD.
Turning off the bedside light, Bitu groaned again.
'Now go back to sleep!'

28

NEXT AFTERNOON, SRI Omo-ji and the Maharaja were
seen taking a long walk through the grounds, greeting
the *punyas* as they went.

It seemed as though they were both happier than
ever, revitalized in some mysterious way.

A devotee from Guatemala disclosed to her husband
that she sensed a new incarnation approaching. Another,
from Mexico, told her daughter she'd overheard the
Maharaja of Patiala declaring his love for life at Pimperne
Hall.

The following night an intruder alarm sounded through
the house, waking everyone.

As the dormitories erupted in commotion, Marney
rushed to the private apartments to check on the godman
and his companion.

Lying in bed in their separate suites, they were
drenched in blood.

Their throats had been slit.

A police report later deduced the assassinations
had been performed by a professional hit-man using a
Jagdkommando knife. The cause of death was of little
interest to the inner circle or the blue faces.

Each one of them was distraught beyond all reason.

Eyes blood-red, his voice faltering, Rosco fell to his knees in prayer. When it was over he suggested they open the packet left in Safe No. 6.

This was done.

Among the detailed notes, funeral instructions were found should they ever be required.

Were either Sri Omo-ji or the Maharaja of Patiala to expire, the notes spelt out, they were to be interred beneath the great oak tree in the Hall's garden. On no account was either of them to be cremated, and the funeral was to be held without delay. A medical examination by a named doctor was to confirm that death had occurred, but an invasive post-mortem to ascertain the cause of death was absolutely forbidden.

The body of the deceased was to be left alone in the hexagonal meeting room until the funeral, the lid to the coffin unfastened until the last moment.

29

AT DAWN NEWS of the tragedy was broken to the *punyas* in the great auditorium.

None of the inner circle or the blue faces had wanted to make the announcement, as if doing so implied they were in some way responsible for the unspeakable loss.

After the drawing of lots, it fell to Marney to be the messenger.

Inconsolable, he stepped up onto the stage, the twin

spotlights illuminating him, video cameras carrying the scene to giant screens on all six walls.

As soon as the audience saw his expression they guessed the message.

'It is my solemn duty to inform our beloved community, and our friends around the world that, at one twenty-three this morning, His Celestial Highness Sri Omo-ji, and His distinguished companion, were found murdered in their apartments here at Pimperne Hall.

'We understand their lives were taken by an assassin who broke in to our precious community. Our prayers are with their souls, and with the guiding light of our beloved Sri Omo-ji, a light of Love and Peace radiating down on us all.'

30

A MASS OUTPOURING of grief at the ashram followed the statement and carried on for many days.

All over the estate, devotees could be found screaming as if mortally wounded, hugging, sobbing, and sitting beneath the trees in silent contemplation. A few took to fresh acts of penance to deal with their pain, although most were so injured already, they refrained from yet more self-harm.

The international press corps rolled back into Dorset, mobile satellite ground stations broadcasting updates worldwide. Remarkably, information relating to the more gruesome acts of penance was suppressed.

The media reported the death of Sri Omo-ji in a respectful and profoundly moving way. So much so that a widespread public grief followed, which surprised hard-nosed media commentators everywhere.

Within hours of the announcement, ordinary people all over the world were talking about the guru's death. The anchor on CNN described it as being like 'a light of Truth and Peace being extinguished'. France 24's newsreader broke down in tears as she read the evening bulletin.

In Britain, flags were lowered to half-mast on government buildings, and church bells tolled in honour of what Her Majesty described in a statement as 'a selfless and exemplary existence'. The Prime Minister went on television to extend his condolences, as did the President of the United States, and more than seventy other world leaders – from Mexico to Mongolia.

The instructions left by the guru were followed to the letter.

The only people permitted to attend the funeral were those who'd been at Pimperne Hall when His Celestial Highness's soul left its mortal body.

Dignitaries, the international press, and tens of thousands of well-wishers who'd turned up at hearing the news were asked to respectfully stay outside the gates.

Three days after the assassinations, plans for the twin

burials were complete. Permissions were granted to site both graves beneath the great oak, the tree Sri Omo-ji had so adored.

As per instructions, the coffins were kept in the Hall's hexagonal meeting room until the funeral was ready to begin.

An hour before the ceremony, the inner circle and the blue faces slipped in and sat meekly on the floor. Unified in pain, they each feared taking on the solemn duty of continuing the teachings of His Celestial Highness.

'How will we ever do it?!' Marney cried in a sudden outburst.

'He's with us,' Rosco offered in comfort.

'They're *both* with us,' Marek said.

Breathing sharply in, Elaine wiped away her tears.

'We'll honour their love, and do justice to the Path of Omo in everything we do,' she said.

31

AT TWELVE NOON precisely, the *punyas* lined the route from Pimperne Hall to the great oak tree at the far end of the landscaped gardens.

Some were weeping, but most were too numb from crying and too injured from self-sacrifice to shed any more tears. Their eyes ringed with woe, they just stood there, like hollow vessels.

A pair of timpani marked the passing of time.

Carried from the house, the coffins were borne

forward on the shoulders of the inner circle. The blue faces went ahead scattering emerald-green rose petals, fingers scented, minds choked in grief.

Ceremoniously, the coffins were lowered into the ground, and the soil was filled in.

Trooping past, the disciples tossed in handfuls of rose petals, while bidding their own personal farewell.

32

AT A GOOD distance from the burial, two old friends were watching from a tree-house in the forest, their expressions sombre.

'Well, that's that,' said one.

'Thought it went off smoothly,' the other added.

'Think we fooled them?'

'We bloody well better have!'

'What if someone figures it out?'

'Figures *what* out?'

'What actually happened.'

'Well, there's nothing stopping His Celestial Highness from mysteriously rematerializing for the Nineteenth Incarnation.'

'Wonder what colour it would be.'

'I was thinking yellow. The Buddhists have done well with it.'

'Yes, yellow... I'll make a note of that.'

Climbing down from the vantage point, the pair of friends crept down into the tunnels and emerged in

Stourpaine. Clean-shaven, they were wearing ordinary street clothes.

They took the local bus to Salisbury and bought one-way train tickets to Blackpool. During the journey they only conversed once.

Harry said:

'You're a genius for cutting the only loose end.'

'You mean Zap?' Bitu replied.

Harry nodded.

'He really thought we were goners.'

'They all did… even the doctor!'

'*And* the police.'

'Damned impressive hoodwinking them.'

Harry grinned.

'Nothing more than basic stage magic,' he said.

33

THAT NIGHT, HARRY and Bitu strolled from the station to Henry Street.

The lights were on at number ten, a Bollywood hit playing loudly inside.

Bitu paused at the gate.

'How d'you think your ma and pa will take you coming back like this?'

'I'm sure they'll get over it.'

'Think they heard about Omo-ji?'

'Doubt it. They're in their own world of Guru Nanak and third-hand lamb chops,' Harry said, before adding:

'Wanna come in?'

'You go in alone.'

'But where'll you go?'

'I'll find somewhere,' Bitu said. 'If worst comes to worst there's always Mrs Jeffries two doors down.'

Harry reached out and hugged his friend harder than he'd ever hugged anyone before.

'It was the greatest adventure,' he said.

'Certainly was,' Bitu replied with a sniff.

'Got to get down to planning,' Harry mumbled.

'Planning what?'

'The new incarnation.'

'No way! Sri friggin' Omo-ji's buried and gone!'

'Don't mean him!' Harry exclaimed. 'I'm not talking about Omo-ji.'

'Then who?'

'The *other* new incarnation!'

'Which one?'

'The new incarnation of the Great Maharaja Malipasse!'

Bitu groaned.

'See you at Mack's for breakfast?'

'Sure, but I'm warning you I don't have anything… not even enough for a fry-up.'

His friend grinned.

'Well that's lucky I kept a little memento of our great adventure isn't it?' he said in the Maharaja of Patiala's voice.

'Memento?'

Turning into the lamplight, Bitu eased up his coat sleeve.

Strapped to his wrist was the Patek Philippe Grandmaster Chime in rose gold.

Finis

Afterword

Godman was born inside me.

I like to think the story grew as I grew, travelled as I travelled, and learned as I learned. As anyone who's read my *Sorcerer's Apprentice* knows, an Indian magician visited our home in the English countryside when I was a child. The guardian of my ancestor's tomb, he was a great hulking Pashtun named Hafiz Jan. While all the other kids I knew were on their skateboards, I was learning magic under his doting gaze.

Hafiz Jan was eventually banished. One of his magic tricks went terribly wrong, and my parents and sisters were almost incinerated by a fireball. The illusions, which were of the type developed by Harry Houdini, and used by India's so-called 'godmen', were based on shockingly dangerous chemical reactions. But for a child in a dull English village, they were the thing of ultimate wonder.

When my beloved Hafiz Jan left, retracing his way back to northern India by land with his tea-crate filled with chemicals, I vowed that one day when I was old enough, I would seek him out and learn the magic of the godmen.

And, I am pleased to say it's exactly what I did.

During the time I was in India learning about magical illusion – journeys that eventually formed the basis of *Sorcerer's Apprentice* – I grasped how virtually anyone with a box of chemicals, and the right spiel, could set themselves up with a livelihood. It wasn't so much about their skill, but rather about the audience's faith.

Or, rather, their need to believe.

Over the years I have witnessed the most extraordinary feats of illusion performed in great halls with devotees numbering in their thousands, and on railway tracks where I was the only person watching. I've been spellbound by performances, and have winced as well, especially when tricks nosedive as they frequently tend to do.

Although I only wrote the manuscript of *Godman* in the last few months, the story came to me on a freezing morning outside Lucknow in the mid-nineties. I had spent the night in a hovel, waiting for a holy man named 'Trapat Guru' to appear. Everyone I had asked waxed lyrical about him, declaring him to be a 'real saviour', as though all the other godmen were nothing at all.

After much waiting, Trapat Guru finally turned up.

The very last person I expected him to be, he was in his thirties, long-limbed and gangly, with a ready smile. But it wasn't his age or physical characteristics that struck me.

Rather, it was his voice.

Until that morning, all the established godmen, or wannabe godmen, I'd encountered were Indian, born and bred. Trapat Guru was quite different. He looked Indian, but had a thick Glaswegian accent.

News of the holy man's arrival spread fast and, as usually tends to happen in rural India, a crowd gathered fast. People streamed from their homes, all milling about, waiting for the action.

Joining them, I watched.

First, Trapat Guru blessed the throng. Then he performed a series of magic tricks – advertised as 'miracles'. After that, he treated about a dozen of the villagers, for everything from aches and pains, to deafness. At the end of the routine, Trapat Guru handed out home-made amulets, and received small donations in return.

I couldn't help but be drawn to him, as though we were two members of a similar fraternity. While I had been learning about magic and illusion from a master in Calcutta because it fascinated me, he was using the same skills to support himself.

In the circumstances, I didn't go over and strike up a conversation, because it risked unmasking him. And, although I didn't quite approve of what he was doing, he was relieving boredom, and didn't seem to be harming anyone.

Instead, I found myself fantasizing a story in which a down-on-his-luck stage magician from England went to the subcontinent, and turned himself into a godman superstar. That's how the story that became my novel, *Godman*, came about.

More interesting though, at least for me, was a second

encounter which took place ten years ago...

I was visiting Scotland for a literary festival, and stayed in Edinburgh for a few days. The city inspires me enormously, because it's where my grandparents met during the Great War.

While in town I looked up an old writer friend, and we went to a pub he'd recommended. A dingy backstreet haunt, it was the kind of place I'd usually be keen to avoid.

But my friend insisted we go there, so we did.

We hadn't been inside for more than a few minutes, when the landlord announced that a magician would be performing. And, without further ado, Trapat Guru stepped out.

Recognizing him at once, I was propelled back to the patch of open ground west of Lucknow. He looked older, of course, but it was unmistakably him. Same ready smile, same long limbs, same thick Glaswegian accent.

This time, I couldn't give up the chance to make contact. So, when the routine was over, I introduced myself.

'I'm Arnie,' he smiled. 'I read your book, *Sorcerer's Apprentice.*'

'I saw you performing near Lucknow,' I said.

'Oh.'

'Was you, wasn't it?'

Arnie blushed, winced, and nodded.

'I never took the donations,' he said, as though he was expecting me to condemn him.

'I'm sure you didn't.'

Arnie leaned forward and pulled a playing card from my ear.

The ten of hearts.

'I'm not a magician at all,' he confided.

'Well, I was impressed by the tricks,' I said brightly.

'That's not quite what I mean.'

'Then what are you if you're not a magician?'

'I'm an anthropologist,' Arnie said.

He explained how he'd spent six months criss-crossing India, doing tricks as a way to study people.

I asked what his conclusions had been.

Arnie looked at me hard, his eyes honest and wide.

'I learned that people need to believe,' he said. 'Whether they like it, they need it, just as they need sunlight, air, and food.'

Tahir Shah

—— A REQUEST ——

If you enjoyed this book, please review it on your favourite
online retailer or review website.

Reviews are an author's best friend.

To stay in touch with Tahir Shah, and to hear about his
upcoming releases before anyone else, please sign up for his
mailing list:

 http://tahirshah.com/newsletter

And to follow him on social media, please go to any of the
following links:

http://www.twitter.com/humanstew

http://www.facebook.com/TahirShahAuthor

http://www.youtube.com/user/tahirshah999

http://www.pinterest.com/tahirshah

http://tahirshah.com/goodreads

http://www.tahirshah.com

Made in the USA
Coppell, TX
24 March 2024

30494632R20146